ELK MEADOWS

****

John Hansen

Dedication:
*To my wife Debi who serves as my editor
and source of encouragement.*

Published through SUMMIT CREEK PRESS

ISBN: 978-1-0878-5750-3

CHAPTER ONE

It wasn't on any map, but those who had spent any time in the country north of Idaho City knew it as Elk Meadows. For some reason, the thick timber that smothered the mountains there gave way on either side of a little spit of a creek that ran through a shallow basin filled with yellow grass. Guarding this utopic depression was gray craggy rock that rose up above the dark forest so steeply that the trees couldn't get a foothold. Before the miners had come these treacherous slopes had been home to bighorn sheep that shared the yellow grass below with the elk. But the miner's appetite for meat had made the sighting of a bighorn or an elk noteworthy, at least in these parts it was.

They'd come into the basin by way of a notch in the rock to the west of them. It was narrow but wide enough that a man on horseback could push a small bunch of cows or horses through it without much effort. In fact, it more or less functioned like a long chute, as even the dumbest of critters could see there was no escape up the near vertical sides of the passageway.

It was an exaggeration, but the words told of Zach's frustration when he said, "There's more damned tracks here than on the Chisholm Trail."

His long-time friend and ranch partner, Able Pascal, came back, "I believe we've come too late to this dance. Them tracks of our horses was colder 'n yesterday's coffee before we come on to 'em and now, with these others thrown into the mix, there ain't no tellin' what we'll find if we ever catch up to whoever is makin' 'em."

Zack looked down slightly as he shook his head and laughed derisively. They had been trailing what they believed were seven of their horses that had been stolen several days ago. It had only been this morning that they discovered the horses were missing from the herd of over a hundred that they were raising to sell to the Army. Looking Able in the eyes, he said, "Ya know, the hell of it is, while we're out here chasin' after these scoundrels there could be others of the same ilk helpin' themselves to the rest of our horses."

"You don't trust Shorty to look after things?"

Zack turned his head to the side and spit a stream of tobacco juice off the side of his horse. Wiping his dark moustache with the back of his hand he sighed, "I'm kinda hopin' if that was ta happen, Shorty would be elsewhere."

Able 's dark eyes shot a look of disbelief towards Zack. "Elsewhere? What are you saying? Why have the old coot around then?"

Zack reined his horse to a stop causing Able to do the same. He said, almost like he resented having to state the obvious, "He ain't no gun hand. These fellows stealin' folks' stock mean business. Shorty 'd just git his self killed if he was ta try 'n stop these hardcases from takin' our horses."

"Well then, I reckon we'll just go broke."

Zack frowned. His first impulse was to come back hard, but he caught himself and softened the tone that he'd loaded on his tongue. "You know what I'm sayin' is likely true. I know you don't want that."

Able's face was shadowed by the wide brim of his gray Stetson. The sweat stains around the base of its crown seemed to give credence to his anger and frustration. He was only 30 years old but already, he had crow's feet at the corners of his eyes. He dabbed nervously with his gloved hand at the right side of his black bushy moustache. "I didn't mean to come off soundin' like I don't care about what happens to Shorty, but dammit, I'm tired ah bustin' my ass only to have some no-account scalawag take it from me."

From their days in the Army together, Zach knew that both Shorty and Able were good men, but in their own right. Able as a cavalry trooper and Shorty as the company farrier. In the early part of his career Shorty had been a good soldier, but several arrow and gunshot wounds and bad falls from horses shot out from under him had relegated him to staying on post and caring for the horses. Even though he was only a year older, Zack sometimes felt like he was talking to Able as a father figure. He came back, "Maybe we should cut our losses with this little bunch and go protect what we've got. We got lots ah work ahead of us. You know the Army is gonna want them horses at least broke to lead."

Anger came to Able's green eyes. "And just let these thievin' sons-ah-bitches git away with our horses?"

It now took some effort for Zack to check his tongue. It was a warm September day. Tiny rivulets of sweat were seeping down both his temples. He sighed as if to forestall responding in kind to Able and removed his Dakota-style Stetson, a gray sharply peaked hat that had less brim than most cowboy's headgear. Holding the hat and his reins in his left hand he ran the fingers of his right hand through his short brown hair in a thoughtful motion. *He knows better than to think I'm a coward.* Zack's horse snorted in a tired sort of way as a Steller's Jay screeched from a big ponderosa pine tree nearby causing a pine squirrel to add his chatter to the quiet of the woods. A twinge of doubt suddenly invaded Zach's mind as he saw from the corner of his eye the holstered .45 Army Colt on Able 's right hip. *I ain't the gun hand that he is but he isn't as handy as he thinks. It's gonna be his undoing someday.* And then Able 's stare from no more than six feet away demanded a response. Zack came back, his blue eyes probing Able 's face. "I say if we don't find 'em in the basin we go home and protect what we've got there."

For a moment Able continued to stare at Zack and then he scoffed. "Alright, we'll do it your way but know this, if we catch up to these thieves I'll not show them any mercy."

The meaning of Able 's words flashed in Zack's mind. He shook his head so as to be barely noticeable and not invite a debate. *He knows better 'n that. Hanging a man these days is likely gonna git us crosswise with the law.* He said aloud in a tone indifferent to the no mercy part of Able 's words, "I reckon then we'll work these tracks till about dark and make camp down here in the big meadow by the crik."

Able nodded. "Some of this sign is fresh, today I'd say, so we best keep a sharp eye out."

Zack eyed the dark green horse droppings scattered in the tracks. All of them were fresh enough to still have a strong odor. Some of them, however, appeared moist while others were dry looking. The horse tracks were different, too. Some looked recent, the dirt within them being soft and crumbly while the soil in others had set up more, probably because of a light rain two days ago. And then, mixed in with the shod tracks were those of horses with no shoes, these were their animals. Unfortunately, they were among the old tracks. Zack came back, "I ain't sure what to make of this sign. It could be Elk Meadows is where these rustlers has come with their ill-gotten gain 'fore they move on to dispose of 'em."

"Might be," said Able in a friendly tone. "Be a dandy place with all the feed and water there is."

Instinctively, Zack brushed his right hand over his holstered Colt 44-40 as if he was heeding the premonition that had come to his mind. "You know it could be these boys might have a trail watcher out here. In these big old trees with all the grass and brush it'd be no trick at all for a fella handy with a carbine to hide his self and then, when we come ridin' along all fat and dumb, he'd just dump us right out of our saddles. Probably be about on par with shootin' fool hens."

"So whaddaya thinkin' we otta do?"

Zack paused briefly as he re-played in his mind the vision of a large caliber bullet smacking him dead center in the chest and violently knocking him backwards out of his saddle, as he did several ravens flying overhead began circling and cackling. Zack looked up at the big black birds and scowled. Their behavior, combined with the pine squirrel and Steller's jay carrying on like they were, announced he and Able 's location which only added to the melodrama in his mind and the course of action he was about to propose. "I'm thinkin' we otta pull off these tracks 'fore we git ourselves bushwhacked. Maybe just skirt the edge of the basin for a ways and then, in due time, we pick a spot where we come back down through the timber to where we can git a good look at the meadow. If these fellas with our horses is here, they likely have got 'em on the best grass and water."

Able looked at Zack like he was reluctant to speak, but then he came out with it in an arbitrary tone of voice that went back to where their conversation had just come from. "You know these fellas likely ain't gonna come along peaceably with us all the way to the sheriff down in Idaho City. You know that don't ya?'

"I guess we'll just see how it plays out."

Able laughed. "Hell, I ain't no fortune teller or such but I'd bet ya my share ah the horses how these hombres is gonna be when we tell 'em we intend to take 'em to the hoosegow."

A look of disgust came over Zack's face. "You didn't git enough killin' in the Army?"

"I didn't kill anybody that didn't deserve it. Same as these guys, They've earned what's coming to them."

Zack glanced at Able but said nothing before nudging his bay horse named Biscuits, on account of his fondness for sourdough biscuits, onward through the towering ponderosa pine. He went no more than about a hundred feet before going off the rustlers' trail and into the trees. The tension between him and Able today was unusual but it came as no surprise in light of the persistent thievery of not only their horses, but other ranchers' stock as well throughout the Boise Basin. It was 1883. Times were tough in the Idaho Territory. Mining gold and silver had lured thousands of men to the rugged mountains in search of their fortunes. It was a boom-bust proposition at best, with little mining towns springing up overnight only to die a not-so slow death. The inhabitants of some of these failed ventures often turned to larceny as a means to live. And so it was that Zack and Able found themselves pursuing an unknown number of them.

Elk Meadows was about a mile long by about a half mile wide. The grass there had escaped being grazed off due to its remoteness and the fact that most men in the area were chasing after gold and not cows. As a consequence of this, the grass was knee high to a tall man in most places. It made for a bucolic setting as Zack and Able visually searched the meadow while staying hidden just inside the edge of the heavy timber. The sun had dipped below the rim of the basin causing a shadow to fall over the woods and valley floor, with one exception. As luck would have it, or God planned it, the sun was now aligned with the notch in the rock allowing a shaft of brilliant soft light to pour out onto the meadow. It penetrated the shadow like some sort of celestial pathway. It was soothing, if not a little mesmerizing, to Zack and Able. The two of them were caught up in looking at the warm haziness of this light and the insects that swarmed in it near the willow-choked creek when they became aware of a horse that had emerged from the willows. It did not appear alarmed or agitated like it was trying to escape someone or something, but rather its focus seemed to be finding new grass.

"It's got a rope around its neck," hissed Zack.

Although they were a good 300 yards away, Able kept his voice barely above a whisper. "I'll bet he's draggin' a picket pin at the end ah that rope."

Zack nodded. "I 'spect he is, but I'm just wondering who's gonna come lookin' for 'im."

Able shook his head in a cautionary way. "Well, whoever it is they must want to stay outta sight pretty bad to camp in them willows with all the damned mosquitoes that's down there."

"I reckon so. Most folks would camp away from the creek and that bug factory and just go to the creek for water as need be."

"Well I suppose if we was ta sit here long enough somebody is gonna miss that horse and come lookin' for 'im. I guess then we decide if they are the ones who stole our horses."

Zack turned his head to the side and spit tobacco juice. "Suits me. It'd be just our luck if we was to go trapesing across this meadow and them ole boys spied us from inside that thicket, we could end up being worm food assumin' somebody cared enough to put us in the ground."

A wry smile came to Able's face. "Well I'm thinkin' since we left the Army there probably ain't no one, 'cept maybe Shorty, that would be concerned enough to give us a decent burial and he'd probably never find us clear out here, so maybe we better just sit on our backsides and let this play out."

Zack was about to continue the friendly repartee between them as a means to heal the tension that had arisen earlier that day when he detected movement at the edge of the willows upstream from the horse. At first he said nothing, as he was peering through the shaft of sunlight coming from the notch in the rocks and into the shadows beyond. But then he whispered, "There's something comin' down the crik."

Able shifted his eyes towards where Zack was looking. "I'm not seeing it."

"Well, they've stopped. They blend in good with the willows."

"Maybe it's a deer."

"There's two or three of them and they're actin' sneakier than any deer I ever saw." And then the willows became too thick to walk through causing the unknown entities to step out of them into the open. "They're men," said Zack excitedly. "First one's carrying a rifle. Can't tell about the other two. It appears they got business with whoever owns this stray horse."

"Judging from the way they're sneakin' up on this camp they must figure they won't be welcome."

Zack sighed as if slightly perplexed. Then he said, tentatively, "Well, I guess nuthin's changed for us. We'll just let these fellas do their business and then we'll go see if any of it pertains to us."

Able sputtered a nervous laugh. "Be like watchin' one of them wild west shows for free."

It seemed to Zack the tension from earlier in the day had healed itself. Things were back to the way they usually were between him and Able. In spite of the potential consequences of what was about to unfold in front of them he loaded the words, *Just need a sarsaparilla and popcorn and we'd be set*, onto his tongue. But before he could project the words a man came out of the willows near the stray horse. He stooped to pick up the rope that the horse was dragging but before he could get it the horse bolted and ran further out into the meadow. The man yelled at the horse in a language neither Zack or Able understood, but one they had heard many times in the Boise Basin's mining country.

"That fella sounds like a Chinaman," whispered Able.

"I 'spect he is," replied Zack as he continued to watch the man try and catch the horse. "He ain't dressed like most of the Chinese you see with those pajama looking jackets, but he appears to have dark skin and he's probably a head shorter than either one of us."

"He's having a devil of a time catching that thing," said Able as the horse broke into a trot going even further out into the meadow. And then he snickered in a low tone. "I don't think this fella stole our horses."

"Nor do I," whispered Zach who was now intent on watching the three men work their way down along the edge of the willows. Nodding towards the men, Zach added, "In about a minute, those boys is gonna have this Chinaman cutoff from his camp in the willows."

"It could be the Chinaman has got friends there."

"That'd probably be good as I don't think these other fellas is comin' to make a social call."

"Ya suppose we otta weigh in on this affair?"

Zack hesitated as he shifted his attention from the three men to the Chinaman and back. He knew of plenty of examples where Chinese had been abused or even killed by white men in the mining country with little consequences. He sympathized with the Chinese but, at the same time, he didn't want anymore trouble than what he already had. And then it was too late.

"Hey Toby, Toby Sing, I know you. Stop right there."

The Chinaman had been completely unaware of the three white men's approach. Shock, then fear, consumed his face as he spun around to face the man who had called out to him. The man was of medium build with short red hair and a thick droopy moustache. He was smartly dressed with a black vest and coat and derby hat of the same color. In his hands he carried a Henry .44 Caliber rifle which he now leveled at Toby Sing.

Toby Sing called out in a faltering voice, "Hello, Mr. Bickers. It is good to see you."

Bickers laughed. "Well it's good to see you too, Toby." And then before Bickers could continue the two men behind him laughed loudly. They were scruffy, hard looking men. Their tone was menacing and evil sounding. As their laughter died down, Bickers went on, "Li Ming has come up missing. You wouldn't happen to know where she is would you?"

Bickers' demeanor was blatantly disingenuous. It caused Toby to become even more fearful to the point his bottom lip began to quiver, still he said, "No Mr. Bickers, I no see Li Ming in long time."

"That ain't what I'm hearing, Toby. A man I know to be honest told me that he saw you and Li Ming sneaking outta town in the middle of the night a coupla days ago. He said she was riding a sorrel horse, kinda like the one over there that yer trying to catch." Bickers paused, smiling at Toby and the recalcitrant horse in an evil way while he waited for a response. And then suddenly, as if he was tired of the game he was playing with Toby, he shouted angrily, "Where is she? Li Ming is mine. I won her fair and square."

Tears had come to Toby's eyes. "The man who tell you this is wrong."

"No Toby, you're wrong to have stolen my property. She's got a debt to work off. Last chance, Toby. Where is she?"

"Li Ming is no whore."

Enraged, Bickers seethed the words, "She is until she pays off her debt."

Because Bickers was standing in the shadow beyond the shaft of sunlight where Toby stood, Zack and Able could see clearly the muzzle flash from his rifle and almost in the same instant they saw the effects of the heavy bullet as it entered Toby's chest and then continue on its way out his back in a shower of blood and fragments of flesh and bone. The impact caused Toby's arms to fly up flailing like pieces of string as he crumpled to the ground without making a sound.

"Well I'll be damned," whispered Zack excitedly. "He just murdered that guy."

"He sure enough did," said Able in a tone of disbelief. "He shot him like he wasn't any more than a coyote or something."

Zack's face showed regret bordering on anger. "I guess we shudda went down there. Maybe tried to settle things down."

Sensing where Zack's emotions might be going, Able sighed as he looked over at him. "It wasn't any of our concern. And it still isn't. A fella can git his self shot poking his nose into matters that don't concern him, especially if it involves a woman, and a whore ta boot."

Zack frowned. "That fella's dead. We cudda stopped it."

Able scoffed. "Well Mr. Do-Gooder, we could be the ones bleedin' out in the grass down there. Just you remember that."

Zack said nothing ceding the verbal ground that had sprung up between him and Able. *He's probably right*, he said to himself. *That Bickers fella is hot-headed.*

In the calmness of the evening, the black smoke from Bickers' rifle was slow to dissipate. It hung in the air before him. And then from it came Bickers' voice, cavalier in its tone, "I won't tolerate no Chinaman lying to me. No sir, I won't."

One of the sycophants, a bearded, chubby man wearing a tattered black slouch hat and dressed in dark pants with a blue cotton shirt who had moved up next to Bickers chimed in, "Ya had no choice, Mr. Bickers. That fella 's got a pistol tucked in his waist. He ain't even supposed to have that. You know how slippery these *Chi-neeze* are. In another second or two you cudda been the one gittin'shot."

Like a moth to a flame, Bickers went to his man's assessment of what had happened, his justification for the necessity of shooting Toby Sing. He seized the words like they were life itself, fore they might be in the event the law became involved. There was excitement in his voice. "That's right. Toby was breaking Idaho law having that gun." Bickers paused and laughed nervously like he was thinking, formulating the scenario of events that he would tell the sheriff if it ever came to that. "I saw his hand move towards that pistol in his belt. I figured if I didn't get off the first shot – why, why I might end up dead."

Suddenly, a woman's scream followed by angry shouting could be heard from within the willows near the creek. The commotion caused Bickers and the chubby man to turn in that direction. The chubby man shouted gleefully, "Sounds like Ed has caught up to Li Ming."

"Well, go help him, I don't want her gittin' loose in all these bushes with nightfall comin' on."

"Yes sir, Mr. Bickers. We'll git her." The chubby man began to run, his belly jiggling as he did, towards the willows and the sound of the voices. Not long after he disappeared into the thick vegetation the intensity and loudness of the voices increased. And then, from this cacophony of aural pain came a guttural shriek louder than anything up to that point. Quickly following this came an even louder outburst. "Why you little bitch. Bite me, will you? I'll show you."

In the stillness of the mountain air, the voices traveled to where Zack and Able lay hidden. The sound of the chubby man's fist striking Li Ming's face, however, did not reach them, only her scream. Zack looked at Able. His eyes radiated disgust with what he had seen and now was hearing. He shook his head. "Whore or not, I can't abide what these boys is likely doing to that woman."

"You know we won't be welcome down there, especially if Bickers thinks we saw him murder that Chinese guy."

Zack nodded. "I know, that's why we'll be carrying our long guns. It'll look natural enough to be totin' a rifle and it'll put us on an even footing with Bickers since he's got one with a shell in the barrel and could likely thumb the hammer back and shoot one of us before we could git our pistols out."

"Alright, I'll let you do the talking," said Able as he flashed Zack a wry smile.

"Fine enough," said Zack returning the smile.

They retrieved their rifles from their horses that were tied further back in the timber. After each of them chambered a round in their Winchester's and eased the hammers down they stepped from the trees into the edge of the meadow and began walking towards Toby Sing and where Bickers stood just beyond him. They'd gone about a hundred yards undetected as Bickers had his back to them when the ruckus in the willows, which had subsided to crying and sobbing interspersed with profanity and taunts from the chubby man and Ed, spilled out into the meadow like some sort of apparition at the edge of the bushes. It was Li Ming who saw them first. The fact that she was dressed as a man in loose fitting pants and shirt did not hide her feminine qualities. She was pretty, being small in stature with long black hair and eyes. Her expression immediately took on a hopeful look even though, for all she knew, the two young men coming down the gentle slope could be more of Bickers' friends. But they had an honest look about them, Zack with his black wool pants held up by dark blue suspenders and a red cotton shirt, while Able had on a green shirt with denim pants held up by a belt. But of the two it was Zack who stood out with his high-topped leather boots, visible because he wore his pants tucked inside them and his six inch leather wrist cuffs with their ornate engraving. He had a certain swagger about him that Li Ming had picked up on.

In spite of the fact that her right eye was nearly swollen shut and her lips were cut and bleeding, Bickers could see the distant look in Li Ming's good eye. At first, he mistook it for indifference but then suddenly he caught on that they were not alone. The realization sent a huge surge of adrenaline through his system as he wheeled around to face the intruders. Immediately, he pointed his rifle at Zack and Able and shouted out, "You boys might wanna stop right where you are. Ain 't nuthin here that should be of concern to ya."

In spite of the fact they had their rifles cradled in their arms with a round chambered, Bickers still had the advantage as the hammer on his rifle was back and his finger was on the trigger. *He'll surely kill one of us if it comes to gun play,* thought Zack. And then Ed and the chubby man drew their pistols and cocked them.

"Zack, they've got the better of us," whispered Able.

Bickers came again. "You boys would be well advised to just turn around and go back to where you come from."

It may have been the adrenaline that made him do it, or maybe it was Li Ming's swollen and bleeding face, but the words escaped Zack's mouth before he had the time to apply common sense. "Like hell we will. We been trailing some horse thieves since about sunup today and wouldn't you know it, right here is where we ended up."

A mix of anger and disbelief flooded Bickers' face. "You calling me a horse thief?"

Zack's heart was pounding at a furious rate, nonetheless, he pressed on, "Well I don't know. So far it appears ta me yer good at killin' defenseless Chinamen and beatin' up their women. Whether or not yer good at stealing horses remains to be seen."

"Why you silly sonovabitch. I should shoot you right now and leave you for the vermin. I ain't no horse thief and that Chinaman there was heeled. He's got a pistol stuck in his waist."

From behind Bickers, Li Ming, who was sitting on the ground in front of Ed and the chubby man, cried out. "He barely know how shoot it. He no threat to you. Why you kill him?"

Bickers did not look at Li Ming, keeping his eyes instead on Zack and Able, but he said loud enough for all to hear,

"I've always been of the belief that if a man has the moxie to carry a gun then he is likely to use it."

Li Ming said nothing as she looked beyond Bickers and Toby's body to Zack. It was as if she was appealing to him to respond for her.

Able looked over at Zack and said in a voice low enough that Bickers and the others wouldn't hear, "Yer gittin' us in purty deep here, Pardner. You know they ain't got our horses and that whore ain't worth gittin' shot over. They'll kill us sure as the sun coming up tomorrow."

Zack sighed. He'd allowed his emotions to get the better of him and now he had little choice, if he and Able wanted to live, but to eat some crow. He looked over at Toby's body. Already, the flies were eagerly feasting on it, swarming over the wound in his chest and crawling in and out of his open mouth and nostrils and eyes. His queue, which he'd kept piled under his black slouch hat had tumbled out and now lay partially in fresh horse droppings. There was no dignity in dying this way, nor would there be for Zack to senselessly fall on his sword and die a similar death in trying to impose some sort of moral justice on a man who wanted no part of it. Zack said as he feigned indifference to the dead Chinaman and the bloodied whore, "Our only interest here is gittin' back our horses. If you ain't got 'em and these folks ain't either then we'll be on our way."

A broad smirk came over Bickers' face knowing that he'd won out, that he'd intimidated Zack. Still, he played along hollering over his shoulder, "You boys see any stolen horses back there in the willows?"

"There ain't but one horse back there," said Ed in a loud voice, "and I reckon he belongs to the Chinaman."

Bickers hardened his stare at Zack as the smirk faded from his face. He said in a cocky tone, "There, that suit ya. Ain't nobody here got yer horses."

Zack nodded his head. "I can see that, so I reckon we'll look elsewhere."

And then Bickers, being the kind of person he was, threw in, "Yer lucky I let you boys ride outta here after insultin' me the way ya did."

An added pulse of anger instantly surged through Zack and Able. Zack glanced at Able who whispered back, "I'll back yer play."

The scenario of how it would be was playing out in Zack's mind's eye. He would drop to one knee thumbing back the hammer on his rifle and shoot Bickers while Able would shoot either Ed or the chubby man. But then he heard it, the shot that Bickers would likely get off. A dead man's twitch on the trigger and then there was a second shot from the one Able didn't shoot. And just like that the drama in his mind became too real. Able went down and then he felt the bullet strike him but there was no pain as it hit him in the forehead. There was pain, however, as he retreated from the drama in his mind and said aloud, "I guess this is our lucky day."

Bickers scoffed like he regretted what he'd offered up. "Go on, git the hell outta here."

Able glanced over at Zack. "We ain't got much choice."

Zack hesitated, looking first at Able and then back at Bickers. And then Bickers called out, "Go on, I ain't gonna back shoot ya."

Zack took a final look at Bickers, making eye contact with him as if to appeal to his conscience, before turning away and starting up the slope to the timber and their horses. No sooner had they started walking when Li Ming cried out, "Please don't leave me here."

This time they could hear the smack of the chubby man's hand as he slapped Li Ming across the face. "Shut up or you'll git worse than that."

Zack stopped almost involuntarily. He was uncertain what he would or could do but before he could turn around

Bickers called. "I'm done foolin' with ya, Mister. You turn around and I'll kill ya. I got a bead drawed on yer back. Yer testin' my patience. In fact, if you don't start walking right now, I'm pulling this trigger. Three – two –"

Zack began walking. The weight of his shame made it difficult to go up the slope.

CHAPTER TWO

They got to their horses and rode well back into the timber and to the south of where Toby Sing lay dead in the big meadow before making a cold camp. On the way there neither talked much about what had just happened. It was like each one of them needed time to assess his role in the events that had taken place. There wasn't much good to say about any of it. Li Ming was Bickers' whore most likely down in Idaho City. Toby Sing had helped her escape that life and gotten himself killed. And then Zack and Able, just minding their own business looking for ordinary horse thieves, stumble upon this depraved troupe and barely come away with their lives at the expense of their egos.

Although they had laid out their bedrolls, neither Zack or Able had gone to bed. Instead, they sat there looking out into the semi darkness. The moon was not full, but near enough so that a person walking slow could make his way through the woods.

"Ya reckon those scoundrels will try 'n bushwhack us tonight?" asked Able.

"I guess ya never know when it comes to people like that Bickers fella," said Zack in a voice barely above a whisper. "I believe that man's moral compass is stuck on Purgatory. I wouldn't put it past him to have second thoughts and sneak out here and shoot us in our sleep."

"Maybe we shudda rode on out through the notch before making camp. We cudda built a fire, had something hot to eat and some coffee. I'll tell ya, I could kill for a cup of coffee right now." And then Able went silent allowing his words to hang in the air between him and Zack, not purposely, but then again maybe he was hoping that what he'd said would cause Zack some guilt over their discomfort from being in a cold camp.

For a moment, Zack remained quiet in the stillness of the crickets chirping and the hoot of a Great Horned Owl off in the distance. In the near darkness he had the luxury of being able to absorb Able 's stare without making eye contact. Finally, he came back, "You remember that time in Montana down there in that Rosebud country when that bunch ah Sioux jumped us and it got real lively in a hurry?"

"Kinda hard to forget that day."

"Yeah, not many days go by that I don't think about it. I see some parts of it, usually the worst ones in my sleep a lotta nights. But ya know what sticks in my mind more 'n anything else that day?"

His reluctance to conjure up what he was certain Zack was referring to caused Able to sigh deeply. It was discernable close to ten feet away where Zack was sitting on the ground with his back against a big downed ponderosa pine. He said, his voice somber, "Dammit Zack, ya need ta let sleepin' dogs lie."

"We shudda never left him."

"We didn't have a choice."

"So says Lieutenant Farley."

Able smacked the ground with a small stick that he had been using to tease the dirt in front of where he was sitting. "McFarland was dead. He didn't feel it."

"I hope he was dead. I sure as hell wouldn't want them savages carving on me or a Turkey Vulture peckin' out my eyes if I had any life in me."

Able scoffed. "So you just tryin' to take my mind off the fact I'm hungry and needin' a cup a coffee or what?" He paused briefly and then added, "Cuz if ya are, I kin think of better things ta talk about."

Zack was hesitant to verbalize what he'd been thinking about. He'd intended to wait till morning before telling Able what he was wanting to do, but he knew that he'd come too far to leave him hanging so he just spit it out, "I think tomorrow we need to go back and bury the Chinaman."

Maybe he knew what was coming or maybe he was so opposed to it that he didn't need any time at all to consider it, but Able shot back like a rattlesnake striking, "Why hell yeah, Zack. That's a fine idea. We kin just ride on over there in the morning. Why I betcha Bickers would be so tickled ta see us that he'd invite us ta breakfast."

Zack waded right into Able's sarcasm. "Obviously, we'll wait for Bickers and his boys to clear out."

"Well, maybe Bickers will bury the Chinaman. Probably make his dealings with the girl more tolerable if he did."

"Probably so, but I don't see Bickers caring much how Li Ming feels."

"So, yer set on doing this?"

"It won't take the both of us."

"You know I won't let you do this by yerself."

"I appreciate the help."

Although he was tired Zack welcomed the dawn as it crept over the far rim of the basin. They slept, as they had in the Army, in two-hour shifts so that one of them was always on guard. The interruptions made for a fitful night when coupled with processing all that had happened that day. But, in all likelihood, there would have been little sleep for either of them had they not shared the watch. Again, they dared not risk building a fire for breakfast so after a dry sourdough biscuit, washed down with a little water from their canteens, they set out for Toby Sing's camp.

A sliver of sun was just peaking over the eastern horizon. Its position was such that the basin was still covered in shadow, but not so much that they couldn't see from their hiding place inside the timber Toby Sing's body lying exactly where he had fallen the day before. The only thing different about it now were the Turkey Vultures that had converged upon it.

Without looking at Able, Zack said in a low voice, "I knew that son of a buck wouldn't bury him. He's rotten through and through."

Able gestured to a spot about two hundred yards to the north of them where the trees bordered the meadow. "Looks like we ain't gonna bury him for a while either."

In the poor light Zach could make out Bickers and Ed standing next to the fire, but the chubby man and Li Ming were not in sight. The possibilities of what this could mean caused his heart rate to quicken. And then suddenly his speculation came to fruition as Li Ming, clad only in her underclothes, came stumbling out of the tree line as if she had been shoved from behind. Seconds later the chubby man appeared. His laugh carried through the crisp morning air. He shouted, "Your turn, Ed."

Bickers then jumped in, directing his words towards Ed. He said, as if he were selling pony rides, "You had yer turn last night. From here on you boys will pay like ever body else."

Ed mumbled something under his breath before waving off Bickers and the chubby man in a contemptuous manner and walked away towards the horses that were hobbled farther out into the meadow.

Zack found himself watching Li Ming more closely than the others as the group began breaking camp in preparation to leave. She did not appear to be crying but more simply resigned to her fate. She had gotten dressed and was helping load the panniers that Bickers' mule would carry.

Seeing that Zack was honed in on Li Ming's movements, Able whispered, "Ya ever wonder how a pretty girl like that got herself hooked up with the likes a that Bickers fella?"

"That's a head-scratcher alright," sighed Zack as he kept his eyes on Li Ming. "I've heard their own parents will sell them to make ends meet."

Able turned his head to the side and spit some tobacco juice before going on, "You suppose they know what their daughter is in for when they do that?"

"I don't know. Hell, I'd rob a bank 'fore I'd sell my daughter off to be a whore."

Able shook his head. "Well, it's a sorry deal. No decent man would want her now."

Zack remained quiet for a moment and then he said, "Ya know, the spot she's in was likely none ah her own doin'."

Able spit again. "That may be, but I don't think I could look at her as marriage material after the likes ah Bickers' boys have had their way with her."

The image of Li Ming writhing beneath the chubby man suddenly appeared in Zack's mind. It was clear and persistent to the point that he questioned himself, *what difference does it make?*

And then Able destroyed the image. He nodded towards Toby Sing. "Something else that's had their way with a person is them vultures and ravens down yonder. It ain't gonna be pretty."

Zack knew all too well from his time in the Army and seeing dead settlers, soldiers and Indians, what would likely greet him when they got to Toby Sing's body. Nonetheless, he came back, "Able, don't feel obliged to lend a hand with this if it doesn't suit ya. I know you been on plenty ah burial details so I won't hold it against ya if you bow out on this one."

Able 's face was a mix of shame and subdued anger that was beginning to reveal itself. He said, somewhat tersely,

"This fella ain't nuthin to us. He's just another Chinamen. I'm not seeing why yer so fired up about doin' this. Hell, we've left Indians for the vultures."

Zack came back quick, his tone sharp. "They was trying to kill us. Toby Sing never done a thing to us. The only person I know that he's wronged is Bickers and for that I'd buy him a drink if he was alive."

Able sighed deeply and looked away briefly before facing Zack. He said, with a weak grin, "Ya know you got a real knack for makin' a fella feel like a shit heel."

Zack shook his head. "I told ya. You ain't gotta help. Hell, you can go take yerself a nap up here in the trees. I'll wake ya up when I'm done."

Able looked beyond Zack to Bickers' camp like he was done talking about Toby Sing. "They got the panniers on the mule and they're saddling up. Won't be long now, I suspect, and they'll be gone."

Zack forced the tension from his face and his voice. He said, "I reckon not."

They allowed Bickers' party to go out the north end of the meadow and into the timber for a good while before they ventured down to Toby Sing's body. The vulture's handiwork was as gruesome as they'd imagined it would be. It was rivaled only by the smell of the corpse which had begun to ripen. They were lucky to find a shovel and pick at Toby's campsite. He was, after all, a miner. There were a couple of wool blankets too, which they used to wrap the body in. At about four feet down they ran out of soil that had been formed over the hundreds of years by the meadow growing and depositing its litter. Zack struck the large rock again and again with Toby's pick causing sparks to fly. Finally, he stood erect gasping for air. "To hell with it."

"I don't believe anybody could ask for more," said Able in a sincere tone.

From within the grave, Zack shook his head but said nothing.

It was close to eleven o'clock when they pounded the wooden cross into the ground at the head of Toby Sing's grave. They had used the laces from Toby's boots to construct the cross from a couple of pieces of a dead pine tree branch. It had taken Zack a good half hour to carve out: *Toby Sing – Murdered by Bickers – Sept. 10, 1883.* The smell of the fresh dirt and the blue asters that were in flower coupled with Toby being under four feet of soil mostly diluted the smell of death in the air, but not entirely, as it seemed to have penetrated their clothes and coated the insides of their nostrils. It even seemed that they could taste death.

When at last they were done, at least in Able 's mind they were, Zack stood beside the grave just looking down at it and then off at the craggy rocks above the timber in the distance. After their earlier differences over burying Toby, Able dared not probe the awkward silence between them. And then sensing how it was, Zack said, "You reckon we otta say some words?"

"Well, I suppose we could but my recollection is the Chinese don't believe in God. They got some guy named Budda that they believe calls the shots, so I wouldn't have no idy what ta say. But I got no problem if you wanna take a crack at it."

It troubled Zack that they might leave without saying anything. He'd been at plenty of burials but never where he'd been the one giving the sendoff. His inner voice shouted out, *You don't even know this guy. What can you say? He don't even believe in God.* But then Zack removed his hat and looked down at the cross. He said, "God, this here's Toby Sing. He was a Chinaman that hadn't done nobody wrong as far as we know so he didn't deserve to die. We hope you got a place for him. Amen."

CHAPTER THREE

The sun had set some time ago causing the evening air to take on a chill that penetrated Zack and Able 's long sleeved shirts. It seemed, as they rode through the shadowy woods, that the usual sentries were less interested in their coming home. Emerging from the tall pines they eased their horses down a gentle slope covered with yellow grass and sagebrush towards a small creek bordered by quaking aspen in the bottom of a broad canyon. A sprinkling of golden leaves suggested fall was not far away. They paused at the creek and allowed the horses to satisfy their thirst before splashing on across it, the water being no more than a foot deep. And then, at last, they came to the well-worn wagon tracks that ran up the center of the canyon. They were tired as were their horses who snorted their fatigue as they plodded up the wagon road side by side.

And then Able broke in over the rhythmic squeaking of the leather in their saddles, "I don't expect Shorty will have any grub leftover from his supper, but I sure as hell hope he's got the coffee pot on."

Zack laughed. "What would you do if you was ta git snowed in with no coffee?"

Able 's voice took on a tone of mock seriousness, "Why Zack Kotter, yer a cruel man conjuring up some evil thing like that."

Zack laughed again as if to acknowledge the return of the usual comradery that existed between them. He came back, "On a better note, I'd be willin' ta bet ya a sarsaparilla that ole Shorty has got a pie or cobbler or some such on hand. You know what a sweet tooth he's got."

Able smiled broadly in the growing darkness. "That and a cup a coffee would go real nice."

They rode on bantering back and forth. Soon they came to where the canyon narrowed down and the aspens had crept all the way across the bottom of it. The night air here was cool, almost cold, but it was of little consequence to them as home was just beyond the shivering trees. Momentarily, they came to where the canyon widened again and the woods gave way to a grassy meadow and their ranch headquarters. To the left was a corral made from lodgepole pine. It had a chute, also made of poles, extending off of it for about 30 feet. Adjacent to the corral was a small pasture surrounded by a barbed wire fence. There were several saddle horses and a milk cow in it. Just beyond the corral and next to the pasture was a barn with clay mud chinking between the logs of its walls. Large double doors were located on each end of the barn. About 50 yards beyond the barn and set off to the right was their log cabin. It had two bedrooms off of one big room at the front of the cabin that served as the kitchen and living area. To either side of the front door was a window, each had four panes of glass that were ten inches square with wooden dividers separating them. The door, made from rough pine boards, stood open. Through the window on the left the pale, yellow glow of a lantern sitting on the table could be seen. White smoke spewed lazily out of the tin stovepipe that protruded from the blanket of tarpaper surrounding it. Owing to the absence of any wind, the smoke lingered above the cabin far longer than usual before losing itself in the night sky.

They were not quite to the barn when General, Zack's black and white sheep dog, came running out the front door of the cabin barking excitedly. Right behind him came Shorty. As his name implied, he was a small, slender man, no more than about five foot six with salt and pepper hair and moustache. He was wearing Army issue black cavalry boots, dark cotton pants held up by suspenders and a collarless long-sleeved gray flannel shirt that was also courtesy of the Army. In his hands, he carried a double barreled 12 Gauge shotgun.

From atop Biscuits, Zack called out to his dog who was now prancing from side to side before him eagerly waiting for him to get down. His voice was giddy, "Oh I know General dog. It's good ta see you too. Yes it is."

And then, from about thirty feet away, Shorty hollered out as Zack and Able dismounted. "I 'bout gave up on you two tenderfoots. Where in the hell have ya been?"

"Elk Meadows," said Zack as he undid the cinch on his saddle.

Shorty came back in a mildly surprised tone. "Elk Meadows. You boys sleep in or did ya git sidetracked along the way?" And then he laughed. "Ya need yer old Sarge along to roll yer asses outta bed?"

Zack sighed, but kept quiet, pretending that Shorty's probe needed no response. As he pulled the saddle and blanket from Biscuits' back, he could see from the corner of his eye that Shorty was looking straight at him as if waiting for his answer. He avoided making eye contact with Shorty and headed towards the open barn doors with his saddle and blanket. *He'll be like a dog with a bone over this*, he said to himself.

"We had ta bury a guy," said Able.

"What?"

"A Chinaman. A fella shot 'im right in front of us."

"The hell you say?" Shorty paused and then came back with the obvious. "Well what'd he do that for?"

"Apparently, this fella that got shot helped this Chinese whore run out on the fella doin' the shootin'."

Shorty shook his head and whistled in a low cursory way like he couldn't believe it. He came back, "Ya got any idea who this fella was?"

Able grunted as he pulled his saddle from his horse and shouted over its back, "He goes by the name ah Bickers."

Shorty instantly came back, "Hyrum Bickers?"

Zack stepped from the barn door and to the side as Able passed with his saddle. Looking at Shorty, he said, "We didn't git no first name. We're lucky ta not be layin' up there in Elk Meadows with that Chinaman."

"Well, it'd be a curse on the country to have more 'n one Hyrum Bickers. That fella is no good. You don't want ta trifle with him."

"You know this guy?"

"I ran across him some years back when I was stationed out in California. Me and some of the boys was out for a good time one night in San Francisco. This Bickers fella was runnin' a seedy bar and sportin' house. It was the kind ah place, ya know, that draws soldiers and sailors to it like a bear ta honey. Well sir, long story short is two of the boys got rolled out back of this place in the alley. Some of Bickers' thugs worked 'em over purty good. It took one of those troopers about ah week 'fore he died in the hospital. Neither the law or the Army did anything about it. Said they didn't have no proof." Shorty abruptly went quiet for a moment and then blurted out, "That's just like the damned Army, don't ya know it."

Zack set a small pail of oats on the ground in front of Biscuits and then began brushing the horse's back as it ate the grain. He was hesitant to speak his intentions on account of the disagreement he and Able had already had over Toby Sing and Li Ming but in light of Shorty's hatred for Bickers, he went ahead. "Those soldiers in San Francisco may git justice if I git my way."

"How's that?"

"I intend to report Bickers to the law."

"For killin' that Chinaman?" asked Shorty somewhat incredulously.

Zack frowned at Shorty. "Yeah, that's what I aim to do. The man Bickers killed didn't deserve it."

"Well, I wish ya luck." Shorty paused and then said, as if he'd lost interest in what they'd been talking about, "I made up a big pot ah beans with bacon and molasses in it. Turning away, he added in a voice that trailed off, "It was mighty good at supper time. I'll set it back on the stove." And with that he ambled off in the near darkness towards the cabin mumbling to himself. "Ah Chinaman no less."

Able stepped from the barn with a brush and a tin gold miner's pan containing some oats. Religiously caring for their horses was a habit he and Zack had acquired in the Army. He'd made only a few strokes with the brush on his horse's back when he picked up where Shorty had left off. "You really think it's a good idea to go to the law over this Chinaman gittin' shot? From the way Shorty tells it, this Bickers fella is somebody whose tail you don't want to twist."

Zack had his back to Able. For a time, he continued brushing Biscuits without speaking like he needed to justify to himself why he was going to the law. When he thought about all that had happened in the meadows, it was the images of the bloodied and bruised Li Ming that commandeered his mind yet he was going to ride all the way down to Idaho City to get justice for Toby Sing. He said to himself, *She's just a whore. Ain't none of this gonna end up good.* But then he said aloud, "I know how some folks look upon the Chinese and I can't say that I agree with that way ah thinkin', but to me that's neither here nor there. This Bickers fella is just pure evil. This country don't need people like him."

"I won't argue that point but we got enough headaches of our own without you invitin' another one."

Zack knew it was faulty logic but it was all he had. "I'll just tell it to the sheriff and then he can do with it as he pleases."

Able laughed sarcastically. "Okay, we'll see how that plays out." And then he laughed some more.

CHAPTER FOUR

The next morning, they were feeling the effects, mostly in their arms and backs, of having dug Toby Sing's grave down to solid rock. But this was not the reason that it was a little past nine o'clock and they were still at the barn and not on their way. Able and Shorty were going to check on the stock, and Zack to see the sheriff. The delay was due to the fact their horses needed their hooves trimmed and new shoes applied. Having been a farrier in the Army, Shorty had been insistent they set up enough of a blacksmith shop in the barn so that he could forge horse shoes. He was busy hammering out a shoe with Zack and Able looking on when Harley O'Keefe, a neighbor who lived about five miles to the west of them, came riding in. He was greeted by General, barking until Zack hollered out, "That'll do, General."

Harley stepped down from his big buckskin horse and tied it to one of the corral poles. Being a man well over six feet, he was clearly visible from his shirt pockets on up to the wide brim of his gray Stetson even before he came around his horse. He called out, "Mornin' fellers."

"Hey Harley," said Zack in a cordial tone. "Whaddaya know for sure?"

Harley sighed. "Nuthin good," he said as he dashed his head to the side in a downward motion as if to emphasize what was to follow. "I caught some old boys yesterday up Copper Creek trying to make off with about a dozen of my calves. They spotted me comin' down off the ridge towards 'em and the sons ah bitches went to their guns. They started shootin' in a way meaning ta kill me. I made for some trees but before I could git there, they creased my horse Tilly, that sorrel mare I usually ride. I put a poultice on her some Indians told me one time was good for such a thing."

"Looks like they 'bout got you," said Able pointing to a bullet hole in the crown of Harley's hat.

Harley removed his Stetson revealing his short black hair and looked at the hole. "I paid ten dollars for this hat just last spring and now look at it," he said, his voice shaking with anger. "The sons ah bitches 'll know better 'n ta fool with me though, as I got a couple ah shots off from behind the trees with my Winchester. I believe I hit one of 'em as his left shoulder curled in towards his chest sudden like. I'll tell ya, I damned sure wouldn't want ta be on the receivin' end of this ole 45-60. She packs a wallop."

Shorty paused long enough in hammering the horse shoe he was working on to ask, "So they didn't make off with any of yer calves?"

"No, but they wudda had that bunch they'd gathered if I hadn't happened on to 'em."

"I reckon you got lucky coming along when ya did," said Shorty as he went back to hammering.

"What'd these scoundrels look like?" asked Zack.

Harley grimaced. "Hell, I don't know. Just yer regular cowhands. They was a good four or five hundred yards away. I know if I'd been shootin' ah .44 like you boys do I wouldn't ah been able to touch 'em."

Zack came back with a grin. "Well Harley, my little ole .44 ain't got the legs that elephant gun ah yers has but I'll tell ya, any feller I'm shootin' at out at that distance would be well advised ta tell the cook he might not be there for supper."

Able and Shorty laughed briefly as Zack, smiling, took out his Bull Durham and papers and began rolling himself a smoke.

Harley moved on. "You know the one thing that I can say about these boys is that one of 'em was ridin' a fine lookin' gray horse."

At the mention of the gray horse, Zack's mind flashed back to that day when Company E, mounted on their gray horses, followed Custer further north on the bluffs overlooking the Little Bighorn River. Zack, on the other hand, rode with Reno to attack the massive Indian encampment in the valley below. It would be several days before he would help bury his friends in Company E. Visions of that day seldom left his mind when he and Able buried Toby Sing.

Observing that Zack had seemingly withdrawn into himself, Able jumped in, "That's good ta know, Harley. We'll keep an eye out for that horse."

Zack came back. "We're much obliged for the information," he said as he struck a match on the hinge of the barn door and touched the flame to his new creation. He drew on the cigarette until it came to life, as he did, he waved the match so as to extinguish it before dropping it on the ground and grinding it into the dirt with the heel of his boot. He added, looking straight at Harley, "Far as I know this is the first that anybody has actually set eyes on who it is that's stealing our stock."

A hint of pride glimmered in Harley's green eyes but then, lest he not be humble, he said, "Well, I'm certain that gray horse ain't the only one of his kind in these parts so it could cause a feller to go up a dead-end trail."

"But that fella you shot," countered Zack, "I dare say he'll be one of a kind, if he lived."

From deeper within the barn, Shorty hollered out, "A man would be foolish to go to a doctor with a gunshot wound. Ain't no doctor gonna treat 'im and keep quiet about it."

Harley came back. "I suppose it'd be good if the sheriff knew these things but he ain't done nuthin yet to catch these rustlers, so I ain't so sure it's worth the ride down to Idaho City."

Zack sighed knowing where the conversation was sure to go. It wasn't that he minded passing on Harley's information to the sheriff, but rather it was the probable fact that he would have to explain his reason for going to Idaho City. It would be like a row of dominoes falling once it came out about Toby and then Li Ming and the speculation that she was a well-used whore. *Harley will want all the details of everything that happened in Elk Meadows*, said Zack to himself. And then from further back in his mind, a nagging voice pitched in, *There won't be a soul in the Boise Basin that won't know that Bickers' men had their way with Li Ming.* Zack glanced over at Able who was looking straight at him. His eyes suggested he was about to speak for Zack. And then the lie rolled off Zack's tongue like warm syrup. "Harley, I got business at the bank down in Idaho City. I could stop by the sheriff's office and tell him about yer run-in with these hombres if ya like."

"That'd suit me just fine," said Harley emphatically. "You might tell ole Snyder that we might not lose so much stock if he was ta show his face up here ever once in a while."

Zack took a long drag from his cigarette, held the smoke in his lungs just briefly, and then spewed it out like it had come from the bellows in Shorty's blacksmith shop. Grinning, he said, "How 'bout I tell Snyder that Harley O'Keefe says he should git off his sorry ass and come uphold the law on Copper Creek."

Harley played along. "You can tell him too that if I have to keep doing his job for him, I'll expect ah check from the county. Be my deputy wages."

Able laughed. "That'll go over 'bout like ah whiskey fart in a crowded stagecoach."

Harley grinned and snorted. "You can tell 'im whatever ya like. I doubt it'll make any difference one way or another."

Zack had laughed along with them, but he was not blind to the fact that Harley was more serious than not. Most of the ranchers in the area had lost cattle and horses to the thieves. So far, no one rancher had suffered a crippling financial loss, but the toll was growing as the rustlers had become emboldened by the fact they'd not been caught until Harley exchanged gunfire with them. Things were different now.

After having chewed the fat for nearly an hour and, in the course of that, arranged for Shorty to shoe five of his horses the next day, Harley came away from the barn wall where he'd been leaning and said in a jovial tone, "Well, I got better things ta do than gossip with you old hens."

Zack, who had saddled Biscuits for the trip to Idaho City was about to leave as well. He said, "Ya headed home?"

Before Harley could respond, Shorty cut in, "Sure he is. That missus ah his has got him on a short picket rope."

Harley looked at Shorty with mock indignation. "I hope someday some old blister lassos you and keeps you hobbled tighter 'n the orneriest mule ever created. You be sure and invite me to that wedding." And then Harley laughed.

To go to Idaho City, Zack would be following the same road as Harley for several miles. He said, looking at Harley, if you've no objection I'll ride with ya till the road forks."

Harley nodded. "Sure, come ahead on."

Seeing that Zack was about to leave, General looked away from the ground squirrel hole where he had been maintaining a vigil and came running. Zack dropped to one knee and put his face close to General's. He looked him in the eyes. "Idaho City is too far for an old dog like you. You stay here and keep the squirrels in check." General responded by licking Zack's face after which Zack petted his head and tussled his ears. "I'll be back tomorrow so you be a good dog."

Able called out. "You talk nice to that banker. Maybe he'll send ya home with a sack full ah money."

Zack made eye contact with Able and paused just long enough to let him know that he appreciated him keeping quiet about Elk Meadows and, in particular, Li Ming. He didn't quite understand it himself other than he felt sorry for her, and Toby too. There were times when he thought he might be attracted to Li Ming, that it wasn't just pity he felt for her, but he quickly reminded himself that she was a whore and that for a dollar she was anybody's girl. But what really troubled him was that in the midst of all this confusion, Katherine, a wholesome girl in Placerville that he'd been courting, seldom came to mind. Images of her were wallowed on by all that had happened at Elk Meadows, but it was mostly Li Ming. He felt guilty for feeling this way but it just came over him like falling snow, there was no way to stop it.

They'd gone a couple of miles sometimes talking, mostly about the weather and the fact they were glad they'd both put up some meadow hay for the coming winter. When out of the blue, like he had read Zack's mind earlier, Harley said, "My missus tells me that yer sweet on Fred Shockley's daughter."

Zack was slightly taken aback. "We're just friends."

"Accordin' to her ma, Katherine sees it as a little more than that."

Zack sighed, but not so Harley would notice. *And here I thought it might be nice to have some company for part of the trip*, he said to himself. He said aloud, "Sometimes women read more into things than they should."

Harley tossed his head back slightly and laughed, his lips barely parting beneath his black walrus moustache. It appeared he was about to say something when his mouth abruptly flung open in a gasping whimper. In that same split-second Zack saw beyond Harley, way up on the ridge, a puff of black smoke. It was so far that the sound and the bullet that plowed through Harley's chest got there at the same time. And in that same crowded second Zack felt a jolt on his right side. There was no time to process the fact he had been shot, as the horror of seeing Harley tumble from his saddle had caused him to jump down from Biscuits pulling his rifle from its scabbard as he did. Both Biscuits and Harley's horse trotted off a short way leaving Harley lying on the road in plain view. Even as he was kneeling down next to Harley it was clear to Zack that he was dead. His eyes and mouth were both wide open and he had that dead man's stare that Zack had seen far too many times while in the Army. Nonetheless, he was about to check for a pulse on Harley's neck when another bullet kicked up dirt just in front of him. Instantly, Zack scrambled off the two-track wagon road and through the knee-high sagebrush to a small patch of young Douglas fir trees that was no more than a hundred feet across. At this particular place in the bottom of the canyon, the little thicket was an oasis of cover in an otherwise sea of sagebrush and grass about two feet tall that ran two-thirds of the way up the side of the canyon. From there to the top were mature Douglas fir trees. Somewhere within these trees was Harley's killer who was now trying to add Zack to that score.

Who in the hell can this be? Who would want to kill Harley and me? said Zack to himself as he worked his way to the far side of the thicket to where he could see out but stay mostly hidden. Taking a knee, he began to search the ridge above him where he'd seen the gun smoke a short time ago. Although it had only been for an instant, the image of that smoke and the Ponderosa pine next to it flashed again in Zack's mind. *Hell, there's those yellow pine right there.* He locked on to the little clump of trees searching it for signs of the shooter. His heart was pounding furiously, even though the intense adrenaline surge of a moment ago was beginning to subside. In its wake, however, was the realization that his right side was wet. He felt of the wound through his shirt. It was tender to the touch and oozing blood. *It otta clot up in a while*, he said to himself. And then he saw movement, something blue. *Most likely he's wearing a blue shirt or maybe a neckerchief.* Zack began to stare at the spot where he'd seen blue until his eyes began to water because of how far away it was. He sighed and shook his head. He whispered aloud, "Shit, it's 450 yards up ta there if its an inch." He smiled when, in his mind, he heard himself telling Harley earlier that morning how he could shoot that far with his .44. And then there it was again. Zack's heart beat even faster as he locked on to the blue immersed in the maze of green far up on the ridge. Resting the barrel on a tree branch he settled the bead of his Winchester's front sight in the notch of its rear site, which if he'd been hold-ing dead on, might have been good at about 150 yards. But, contrary to his good-natured braggadocio of that morning at the barn, he didn't routinely shoot this far with his .44 and wasn't certain how high to hold. Zack took a deep breath and exhaled slowly as he rocked the heavy octagon barrel upward to where he guessed he was holding about three feet over the sliver of blue that was still visible. *That poor fool thinks he's hid.* And then he took a shallow breath letting it slowly escape as he applied more and more pressure to the trigger. Ka-Boom. The Winchester jumped back into Zack's shoulder as the 200 grain bullet went on its way towards the patch of blue. Moments later the blue disappeared and two bullets, fired almost simultaneously, came crashing through the smoke above where Zack now lay on the ground and buried themselves in the trees. "Damn," hissed Zack aloud. "Sounds like there's more 'n one of those guys. I better be movin. Those scoundrels has honed in on my rifle smoke." But before he could move another shot rang out and then another and another. "Sonovabitch, those boys aim ta kill me," said Zack aloud. And with that he rolled three times to his left before getting on his feet and running about 20 feet to a large tree. He dropped down behind it, trying hard to catch his breath. He was frustrated. He obviously hadn't killed, or for that matter even hit, the man wearing blue. It appeared all he had accomplished was give away his position and antagonize the shooters on the ridge.

Zack sat with his back against the tree, not even facing Harley's killer. He took several deep breaths, holding each one for a few seconds before exhaling. *There ain't gonna be no gittin' outta this little thicket as long as they're up there,* he said to himself. *Sure as I try, they'll shoot me down.* After a few minutes, when his heart and breathing had slowed, he became aware of a Meadow lark singing. And then a Mountain Chickadee chimed in, and for a brief moment, Zack seized the tranquility as a sign that everything would be ok. He began to fantasize how he would escape. *From the edge of the trees I'll crawl on my belly through the brush until I git close enough to sprint ta Biscuits in a second or two and then we'll high-tail it outta here,* he said to himself. But then, as he played that scenario out in his mind, it did not go as he'd planned. He made it to Biscuits ok, but he no sooner got on him and they shot Biscuits out from under him and then they shot him as he struggled to free himself. *Those sons ah bitches have just plain got me outgunned,* he said to himself. *They got buffalo guns or some such.* But then a good thought came to Zack from somewhere deeper in his mind. *Time ain't on their side. They committed a murder here so they'll be wantin' ta put distance between them and Harley.*

It had been about 15 minutes when Zack heard the sound of horses coming at a gallop from up the road. He got to his feet but remained slightly crouched over in deference to the possibility Harley's killer was still on the ridge above. The horses were almost even with the pine thicket when Zack heard Able call out, "There's Biscuits."

Ravens had already discovered Harley. The realization of what he was looking at suddenly struck Shorty, he hollered, "There's a body in the road."

They drew their pistols even before they jumped down from their horses. And then Zack shouted from the edge of the trees, "Git on over here. There's some bushwhackers up on the ridge."

Able and Shorty began to run towards the trees, weaving in and out amongst the sage. Within seconds they arrived at the thicket gasping for air. Able was first to speak, "You got somebody shootin' at ya from the ridge?" he asked in between breaths.

Zack shook his head slightly and sighed. "I did have but I suspect they have vamoosed since you boys didn't draw any fire. But it couldn't ah been long ago if they did."

"Maybe we can catch up to 'em," said Able.

"I'm of the opinion that'd be a long shot," said Zack, "but I'm willin' ta try."

Able 's eyes suddenly fell to Zack's bloodstained shirt. He nodded toward it. "Can you sit a horse?"

"I believe I can."

Shorty sighed. "I reckon that leaves me to take Harley on home."

Zack and Able exchanged glances knowing what an emotional, gut wrenching task it would be to take Harley's dead body draped over his saddle home to his wife and kids. But there was also the matter of getting justice for Harley.

Zack said in a solemn tone, "We'll help ya load Harley on his horse."

The three of them stepped from the trees and started towards the road. Part way there, Zack stopped and looked up at the trees on the ridge for blue. He half expected to see another puff of smoke and a bullet come whistling his way.

"Helluva shot from up there," said Able.

Zack came back, "Harley was dead 'fore he hit the ground."

Shorty spit tobacco juice. It landed on a clump of purple asters that a couple of bees were working on. The impact of the black spit caused them to take flight. Shorty looked up and said, "It boggles my mind how men can be so downright cold-blooded."

"They're the most ruthless animal in the woods," said Zack. "Bears, cougars, they're predictable but man, he's a sorry cuss. Ya never know what he'll do."

As big as Harley was, it was not easy loading him on his horse in a manner that was respectful and not like he was a sack of grain. His horse that had carried him a thousand times before, now became skittish.

"He don't like the smell ah death," said Zack.

"If he falls off, I'll play hell gittin' him back on by myself," said Shorty in a thinly disguised plea for one of them to come along and break the news to Harley's wife and kids.

"It ain't but a coupla miles," said Able.

Shorty frowned but said nothing as he took up the reins of Harley's horse and began leading it towards his own.

Zack wanted to call out to Shorty but could not think of anything to say that would make his errand any more tolerable. He knew there would be no easing the pain of the widow O'Keefe and her two kids, at least not today there wouldn't.

Had they wanted to gamble with their lives, Zack and Able would've ridden straight up to where the killer had been hiding in the trees, but they did not. Instead, they rode up the canyon about a half mile to a shallow, wooded draw that cut into the ridge. After going as far as they could on horseback through the thick trees they dismounted and left their horses, proceeding on foot. They had gained the top of the ridge and were slowly and quietly working their way over to where the bushwhackers had been.

It had occurred to Zack, and he supposed to Able as well, that they were being overly cautious, but Harley was the second dead man they'd had to deal with in as many days. He couldn't deny that being up close to death changed a man's approach to an event that might bring it upon himself. Regardless, there would be no sneaking up on the killers as the Steller's jays and pine squirrels had gone off and they were a good hundred yards from the killer's location. Able looked over at Zack and frowned. Zack shrugged and whispered, "Only a fool would've stuck around this long."

Able came back, dead serious, "Or somebody so set on killin' ya they'd just lay there, quiet as a mouse and let us walk all fat and dumb right into an ambush."

Zack grinned, mainly to boost his own confidence, and said, "Well then, I reckon we better keep a sharp eye out."

Able forced a smile and shook his head before turning away.

They moved on, their eyes searching for anything out of place and, at the same time, trying to not step on a pine cone or twig that would be akin to shouting out, *here we are*. They held their rifles waist high with a round chambered and fingers lightly resting on the trigger. They were coiled as tight and ready as a mountain lion about to pounce on a deer. On they went, one carefully placed step at a time. For Zack, it was more personal, the blue man and his friend had tried to kill him. And, he'd had to endure seeing Harley die, one minute full of life and the next laying on the ground, his dark red blood discoloring a clump of yellow grass. And then at last they were there. Zack made eye contact with Able and nodded towards a big Ponderosa pine just ahead. He whispered, "That's where they were shooting from."

Able turned back to the tree. He studied it and the area around it for a moment. Seeing nothing, he said in a near normal voice, "I believe they've gone on their way."

Zack scoffed and began walking towards the tree. "That would be like them, the cowardly bushwhackers that they are."

They slowly descended upon the shooter's nook, their rifles at the ready. And then there it was, so perfect, a downed tree for the shooter to rest his rifle on and a tree screen in front of it except for one small tunnel of view through the jumbled morass of branches that provided a clear shot at anyone on the road below. As the image of the assassin lying there next to the log sighting on Harley played out in Zack's mind, a shiver ran up his spine. He said to Able, "Ya know, this whole affair has got me wondering just who these boys was wantin' ta kill, me or Harley?"

"Maybe they wanted to kill ya both and rob you."

"Why not just hide in that little patch ah trees I was in?"

Able paused for a moment as if visualizing the trees and then he came back, "Not enough cover for their horses."

Zack nodded his head. "Maybe so." And then his eyes widened as he took a step towards the shooter's rest and knelt down on the ground. Just barely protruding from beneath the log was an empty shell casing. He picked it up and looked at the caliber stamped on the end of it. ".44-100. I knew this scoundrel was shootin' somethin' powerful." And then in the next instant, his mind's eye went back to a short while ago when they loaded Harley on his horse and the gaping hole in his back where the bullet had come out. He had offered up his rain slicker to tie over Harley so the big, bloody hole would not be the first thing Harley's widow saw when Shorty came riding into her yard.

"I've heard ah those," said Able. "In fact, I heard Custer had one but I can't say that I ever saw it."

"I saw it," said Zack. "Fancy damned thing. A Remington single shot. Had ah folding peep sight situated behind the action on the stock. It was a gun only an officer could afford. I betcha there ain't many of 'em in these parts."

Able nodded. "Probably not." And then he stooped over and picked up an empty shell casing that was different from the .44-100. He recognized it right off but read aloud the stamped imprint on its base, ".45-75."

A knowing look came to Zack's face. "That fits ah Winchester lever gun. It musta been that sonovabuck that snapped off three shots at me just as quick as ya please."

"Most likely," said Able, "but I betcha it was the fella with the Remington that shot Harley. That kind a gun is better suited to shootin' that far."

"I suspect yer right."

"Appears they had plenty ah time to plan for it," said Able looking down at the ground. "They got this pine duff all churned up like ah coupla hogs."

"Yeah, it looks as if they made themselves right ta home here in the shade ah these big old pine trees just waitin' for me and Harley ta come ridin' by."

"Well, it puzzles me how these fellas knew you and Harley would be by here at this particular time."

Zack sighed and shook his head. "No, it don't make sense unless these scoundrels were just intent on shootin' whoever come by figuring that they would then ride down to the road and pilfer the bodies of money and valuables and be on their way."

"Maybe that was their plan," said Able nodding towards the backside of the ridge. "They might ah figured that if things went sour on'em they could just bail off here down in ta all that timber country. If those boys knew what they was doin' it'd sure be easy enough ta shake off somebody trailin' 'em."

As much as Zack didn't want to admit it to himself, it was not looking good for he and Able to catch up with Harley's killer. Still, his conscience wouldn't allow him to not go on. "They probably tied off their horses somewhere down here, he said as he began walking and pointing to the heavy timber on the north side of the ridge. Able fell in behind him. They'd gone about fifty yards, taking them out of the relative openness of the Douglas fir and Ponderosa pine trees on the ridgetop to where the slope broke off steeply into the canyon below. Now, the trees were lodgepole pine as thick as any Zack had ever seen. It was a mature stand with lots of trees that had been killed by insects and blown down at one time or another. It was impossible to walk a straight line and stay on the ground. Instead, they found themselves continuously having to step over trees or tightrope walk along at least a portion of their length to get to a point where they could jump down on the ground again.

After they'd gone a short way but far enough for reality to take hold, Able called out, "Ya know, once we git through this doghair crap there ain't gonna be no guarantee that we'll find where they tied off their horses and their tracks outta begins."

Zack stopped on top of the log he was currently balanced on and looked around. It was a sea of green and brown of the living trees and gray of the dead. His unobstructed view in any direction was no more than 20 to 30 feet. It was a sobering check of their situation, he came back, his voice bitter and dejected, "I suspect we may be pissin' in the wind."

Able hesitated briefly but then said, "It's yer call, Zack. Yer the one who's been wronged the most here."

Zack, who was facing away from Able scoffed and said to himself, *Sure put quittin' on me. Folks 'll second guess it.* He could feel Able's eyes on his back. Nonetheless, for a long awkward moment he stood there on the log listening to the eerie roar of the wind rushing through the tops of the trees that swayed to the east with each gust. It reminded him of a distant waterfall. Finally, he turned toward Able. He said in a defensive tone, "There'll be those that ain't here seein' how it is that'll question our not goin' on."

Able came back quick. "Ta hell with 'em. I'm of the belief that our tromping through this jungle will come to no good end. Them boys has got too much of a head start. They make it over to the road goin' ta Placerville, it'll be a tall order sortin' their tracks outta all the comin' and goin' on that road."

Zack's conscience eased somewhat knowing that Able was like minded in not going on. "We got ta git the law involved."

"I reckon we do."

"I believe my time would be better spent going to Idaho City and fetchin' the sheriff."

Able looked to the blood on Zack's shirt. "You sure you don't want me ta go?"

Zack shook his head. "I'll stop in Placerville on my way and have that sawbones there take a look at it."

Able smiled. "Why if I was you, I'd let that purty gal ah yers tend to yer wound."

For a moment, Zack seemed tongue-tied but then he said abruptly, "It ain't that way between us."

Able laughed. "In my opinion you'd be foolish not ta make it that way."

"I took her to a dance and then another time we went on a picnic," said Zack with some edge in his voice. "Now folks has got us marching down the aisle. I ain't nowhere near that."

Still grinning, Able came back. "Just think ah the fringe benefits there'd be on those long cold winter nights."

Zack shook his head and sighed. "I reckon there's lots ah folks that'd call me stupid for not taking up with a pretty girl like that, but its kinda like pumpkin pie on Thanksgiving. Ever body likes pumpkin pie, or so a person would think, but ever once in a great while there'll be ah fella come along that don't like it. I guess I'm that fella."

"You don't like her?" said Able incredulously.

"I like her just fine as a person, but I don't see myself having kids and growing old with her. Besides, she's a town gal. I don't think she'd cotton ta livin' out on a ranch."

Able snorted and tossed his head back slightly. "Well, all I can say is you otta acquire a taste for pumpkin pie."

Zack frowned. "We better head back. I want ta make it ta Idaho City 'fore dark."

CHAPTER FIVE

They had ridden together till they came to the fork in the road. It was not lost on Zack what he was asking Able to do. The fight on the Bighorn and what followed after it, with burying the dead and trying to console family members once they got back, haunted their nights. They'd had enough grief and tears to last them ten life times, but yet here they were again. "Shorty 'll be glad ta see ya," said Zack.

Able sighed deeply knowing what awaited him at Harley's place. He turned his head and spit a stream of tobacco juice into the sagebrush at the edge of the road before coming back in a near sullen tone, "I suspect he will."

Zack picked up on Able 's demeanor but he did not go there. *Ain't nobody envies a person trying ta console a grieving widow and her kids but it can't be helped.* He said aloud, "You can tell Mrs. O'Keefe that I'll let the preacher in Placerville know what has happened. I'm purty certain she belonged to that little church of his. He'll likely come out to the place and help her plan the funeral."

Able nodded. "That'd be good."

Zack gathered his reins a little tighter as if he was about to turn Biscuits down the road to Placerville, but then he paused. He said with a smile while looking straight at Able, "It's been a miserable two days, ain't it?"

Able said, his expression still somewhat solemn, "It sure as hell has."

Still smiling, Zack said, "Maybe when all this nonsense has run it course, I'll stand you and Shorty to a drink in town."

Able snorted and then he laughed. "I'm thinkin' we ought ta just go on a bender."

Zack parroted Able 's laughter. "Keep an eye out." And with that he nudged Biscuits into a canter towards town.

It was about an hour's ride to Placerville. Had it been 15 or 20 years ago, during the town's heyday, Zack's trip might have been over. But now with many of the gold and silver mines played out, the town was a fraction of its former size. It had a city marshal but his jurisdiction was limited to just that, the city.

In spite of all that had gone on that morning, Zack could not shed the images of the day before in Elk Meadows. He found himself having to crowd Harley's lifeless body on that stage of horror in his mind right next to Toby Sing with Li Ming's bloodied and battered face presiding over them. Bickers' voice, counting down to when he would shoot Zack, was echoing just off stage as he rode down Placerville's Main Street. He was coming to Katherine's father's store. Several people had already noticed his bloodstained shirt. One woman going so far as to point right at it and cringe. Zack simply nodded to her as if to say, *Good afternoon,* and continued on. And then there she was, helping a woman carry the goods she'd just purchased out to her buggy. It was the woman who saw him first. She started to turn away, but then she caught sight of the blood and began to stare causing Katherine to follow her eyes. She called out, "Zack, what happened to you?"

Zack made eye contact with Katherine, trying his best to hide his reluctance to talk to her. Nonetheless, he could see in her face that she sensed it was only by accident that she had seen him. Still, she hastily placed the items she was carrying in the woman's buggy and started towards him. As she drew near Biscuits, she stated the obvious, "You're bleeding. What happened?"

Zack brought Biscuits to a halt but did not get down. He came back, "We got bushwhacked."

"We?"

"Me an' Harley O'Keefe." And then, knowing that she would ask, he added, "Harley's dead."

The owner of the buckboard, a middle-aged woman with dark hair falling from beneath her yellow sun bonnet, gasped, "Oh, poor Mabel. And her kids. What will they do?"

Katherine glanced over at the woman as if she was an intruder to what might have been a more personal interaction between her and Zack. She stepped closer to Biscuits and looked up at Zack. "How bad are you hurt? Can I help you?"

Recalling what Able had said, Zack was tempted to say yes but then the naysayer in him shouted out, *there'll be consequences to that*, so he said, "I appreciate it but I'm on my way to see the doctor."

"Will you stop by when you're done there?"

Zack looked down at Katherine. She was pretty with green eyes and auburn hair. Her buxom and shapely figure was clearly evident, despite wearing an ankle length brown cotton dress. He couldn't explain for certain why he felt the way he did, maybe it was just liking his freedom, but he said, "I don't think so. I'm going on to Idaho City. I've got to see the sheriff."

Disappointment came to Katherine's eyes and then it bled into her voice, "Oh, well, maybe on your way back?"

"Yes, maybe on my way back."

It occurred to Zack that Katherine would smile at his response, but she did not. He rode on.

CHAPTER SIX

It rankled Zack that old Doc Holten charged him a dollar to clean his wound and put seven stitches in his side. For some time he dwelled on it as he rode towards Idaho City, but finally had to concede to himself that there had been occasions when he'd spent a dollar on a glass of whiskey and that the stitches would probably do more good than the whiskey. Pastor Morgan, on the other hand was free, at least to Zack he was. And he had assured Zack that he would be leaving within the hour for the O'Keefe place.

Idaho City was situated at the confluence of Mores and Elk Creeks. Before the miners had come the mountains surrounding the town had been covered with Ponderosa pine but now, they were dotted with stumps and slash. Along the creeks were huge piles of tailings from the hydraulic mining operations that had channeled water from the creeks into large nozzles that systematically washed the soil away from the hillsides exposing the gold bearing gravel. To Zack, the land appeared tired and all used up. Nonetheless, as he rode along, he couldn't help but notice the numerous Chinese still working, even in the rapidly approaching darkness. Some had lit pine pitch torches or built fires to better see the gravels in their sluice boxes. They would shovel the already worked tailings into the sluice and then stand over it intently looking for the meagre amounts of gold to settle out. It was cold, wet work. Some took notice of Zack as he rode by, most did not. Of those who did, Zack waved or sometimes nodded. The Chinese generally waved back. *Damn*, he said to himself, *that don't hardly look like a payin' proposition but I guess it's all they can git with the laws being the way they are.*

By the time Zack got into the town proper, lights were visible in most of the buildings, at least those that were occupied. There were a variety of log, clapboard and stone structures. Light blue smoke hung over this assemblage as people finished cooking their supper or stoked fires to ward off the evening chill. Zack reined Biscuits to a halt in front of a large log building not far into town. A wooden sign with dark lettering above its door, read: COUNTY JAIL. There were bars on the windows to either side of the door. Pale yellow light emanated from the window on the right. He could see the chimney lantern from which the light came. It was sitting on the corner of a big wooden desk. A man appeared to be reading. Zack went inside. The man behind the desk looked up, his expression radiated some concern. "What can I do for ya?"

Zack had met Sheriff Herb Snyder before and this wasn't him. He glanced up to a clock on the log wall. It was encased in dark hickory wood. A brass pendulum swung methodically below it metering out the time. Just above it, a glass cover revealed black Roman numerals on a field of white. Zack read the time, *8:05. Hell, Snyder's probably gone home.* He said aloud, "The sheriff around?"

The man behind the desk was much older than Zack, or for that matter, Sheriff Snyder too. He had gray hair that was thinning badly and an unkempt gray moustache. He was wearing a tan cotton shirt and a black vest that was unbuttoned exposing the DEPUTY part of his silver colored badge which was pinned to his shirt. In his hands, he still held a dime western novel that was open. Dog earing the page he set the book down on the desk amongst a clutter of papers, a heavy white coffee cup with considerable stains down its side and an over-flowing ash tray. He came back in a tone that suggested he was a little insulted that Zack hadn't told him what his problem was, "The sheriff's tendin' ta business. Can I help ya?"

Zack suppressed a pulse of aggravation as he shifted his eyes from the deputy to the gun rack on the wall behind him. There were three Winchester lever action rifles and one Winchester pump shotgun standing upright. There were boxes of shells for them on the shelf just below. Coming back to the old man, he said, "I got ah coupla murders to report."

Instant shock registered on the deputy's face. "Murders?"

Zack glanced down at the empty chair to his right. He noted the deputy's watery brown eyes had followed his, but he said nothing. Still standing, Zack went on, "Yesterday, a fella named Bickers shot a Chinaman by the name ah Toby Sing up in Elk Meadows. You know the place?"

The deputy appeared a little numbed by what he'd just heard. His eyes reflected the glow of the lantern but, more than that, they appeared to Zack like the old lawman was elsewhere in thought. It was like he'd become angry and was struggling to contain it. And then he returned, "I know it. Used ta hunt there 'fore the country went ta hell, but you probably ought to talk to the sheriff about this."

Zack was taken aback slightly at the seeming change in attitude of the deputy. Nonetheless, he did not question it and nodded, "Alright, I'll do that but this other matter concerns me an' Harley O'Keefe gittin bushwhacked this morning a little east ah his place."

"Harley's dead?"

"He is and I got ah purty good crease under my arm," said Zack gesturing towards his wound which was not evident due to the pastor having given him a shirt. "Another coupla inches to the left and I'd probably be laid out next ta Harley."

The deputy shook his head. "Did ya git a look at who was doin' the shootin'?"

"No, they was hid purty far off on top of a ridge. But I can tell ya that one of 'em was shootin' a .44-100 and the other a .45-75."

The deputy frowned slightly. "Ah .44-100? I ain't never heard a that gun."

"I reckon a lotta folks haven't. It's a single shot with fancy sights and it ain't cheap."

"So, you ain't got no idea who might want ta kill you and Harley?"

Zack sighed and shook his head. "Harley had a run-in with some rustlers a few days ago. He shot one of 'em but the fella got away. I don't know, maybe that guy."

The deputy stood up and started across the room past a closed door that led to jail cells and then past a row of honey oak filing cabinets along the wall to a stove with a coffee pot sitting on it. He called out over his shoulder, "Ya want a cup?"

"That sounds good. I ain't had a thing since 'fore the chickens was up this morning."

A small open face cupboard that had been painted a pale green with little swirly red flowers sat along the wall to the left of the stove. On the shelf that was eye level with the deputy were more cups resting upside down on a strip of red and white checked oilcloth. He selected a heavy brown porcelain one with a chipped handle. "Sugar?"

"Black 'll do."

Zack watched as the old man's trembling hand set the brown cup on the desk next to his own and begin to pour the coffee. He was almost done when he finally became aware, or maybe he was all along, that Zack was still standing. He said, almost like Zack should have known enough to sit down before now, "Have a seat."

And then he started back across the rough plank floor with the coffee pot. For a moment, the room went quiet save for the ticking of the clock on the wall and the snapping and popping of the pitchy wood in the stove. The deputy was nearly back to the desk when he said in a tired voice, "The country's gotten plum wicked. I always liked ole Harley."

"Yes sir, he was a good man," said Zack as he reached for his coffee. "He wasn't deservin' ah being shot down like that."

The old deputy raised his cup to his mouth and strained a noisy sip of the hot coffee through his thick bushy moustache. "So ya think it was rustlers that killed Harley?"

"I can't think of anybody else that'd have it out bad enough for him to wanna kill 'im."

The deputy snorted and tossed his head back slightly. "For some folks it don't take much cause to kill someone."

"I reckon that was how it was with this Bickers fella shootin' the Chinaman up in Elk Meadows. There was no need for it."

The deputy made eye contact with Zack but then purposely took another drink of his coffee as if he needed the time to formulate his response. It was a three-slurp drink and then finally he lowered the cup. There were several drops of coffee clinging to his moustache. One of the drops suddenly gave way and fell into the gray stubble on his chin. He seemed oblivious to it as he said, "You should know that there's been more 'n one occasion that the sheriff and Bickers has shared a drink."

"So, they're friends?"

"Bickers packs weight in this town. He owns the Ore Chute Saloon." The deputy paused to laugh and then went on, "Hell, he's probably takin' as much gold outta these hills as anybody. These poor fools bust their backs out here on these claims and then they give it to Bickers for watered down whiskey and sportin' girls."

Images of the Chinese working the played-out tailings as he was coming into town came to Zack's mind. He said, "The Chinese too."

The deputy snorted and grinned. "Naw, most ah them is smarter than that. They're out workin' these claims that the white man has give up on cuz he don't think its worth his while but, the Chinaman, he gits a bunch of his friends together and they just keep pluggin' away at it and they make it pay. It ain't a lot but they git by. They ain't got no choice really cuz the law won't let'em file on a claim that ain't never been worked first by a white man."

"That don't seem right," said Zack.

"Probably ain't, but the white miners is citizens and they make the laws. The Chinese ain't got no say."

It suddenly became clear to Zack why the deputy had told him to talk to the sheriff about the Elk Meadows affair. *Might be a waste a time*, he said to himself, *but if the man's got a conscience maybe it'll agitate him enough ta do something*. He said aloud, "So, what time does the sheriff usually show up here in the morning?"

"He's generally here by seven o'clock. He helps me feed the prisoners breakfast."

"So, yer the cook too?"

"Ain't nuthin' fancy. Generally, for breakfast they git mush and a biscuit with some coffee." The deputy paused and then went on with some pride in his voice, "We got 14 cells but right now only six of 'em is occupied."

Zack tilted his cup up and drank the last of his coffee. He set the cup on the desk in a manner that suggested he was ready to leave.

"My name's Nephi Quinn," said the deputy standing and extending his right hand across the desk.

Zack took hold of the man's hand and shook it in a firm way. It felt of callouses from a time, he supposed, that the deputy had been a miner. "Zack Kotter."

"Pleased ta meet ya. I work nights so if yer ever in need of a free cup ah coffee and some bullshit, stop in." And then he laughed studying Zack's face to see how his offer had been received.

Zack laughed back. "I don't git ta town too often but we got a place out on Quartz Creek. So, if you happen ta be out that way swing by. You'd be welcome ta spend the night. We generally got a pot ah beans on and sourdough biscuits in good supply." And then Zack smiled in a wry way. "Probably even rustle up a jug for a snort or two."

From the jail Zack went on to the livery stable and, although he paid the man the four bits he required up front, Zack took care of Biscuits himself. He grained, brushed and made sure he had water before leaving to find a place for him to stay and something to eat. Some things he learned in the Army were just the right thing to do.

It was full on dark now, there being no moon. The man at the livery had pointed up the street to where it intersected the road coming into town. It was a dusty thoroughfare, littered with horse manure, that had become Main street. Most of the viable businesses in the dying community were to either side of it. It was the lifeblood of the town, such as it was. *Turn left there*, he'd said. *The hotel ain't far down thataway*. Although he'd been to Idaho City before Zack had never spent the night there, that cost money. It was free to just start for home and find a place along the way to throw his bedroll out. But that was not the case tonight.

The Skinner Hotel was a white two-story structure with a front porch that ran the width of the building. Three steps about six feet wide provided access to the landing. Ornately carved wooden columns supported a weathered roof above it. There was a dim glow of light coming through the frilly yellow lace curtain on the window to the right of the door, otherwise the establishment was dark. Zack was about to step up onto the porch when a voice sounded in the darkness to his left. "Watch yerself. She's a cranky old blister." And then he laughed briefly as he re-inserted the end of a long-stemmed pipe into his mouth and drew on it several times before spewing the smoke out in front of him.

In the darkness, Zack could not make out much about the man other than he sounded old. He came back, "Thanks for the warning."

"The old bitty ought ta be glad she's got anybody stayin' here at all. Things ain't the way they used ta be. Ain't never gonna be either. Most of the white folks with any sense has moved on. It's just us dumb fools and the Chinese that's stayed."

Zack stared at the outline of the man in the rocking chair. It was moving gently back and forth. It came to him, *the old woman inside isn't the only one who's bitter*. He said aloud, "Have a good evening, Sir." And with that he opened the front door as the old man mumbled something that Zack pretended to not hear.

The lobby counter was situated to the right of a hallway, with rooms on either side, that ran to the back of the building. To the left of the counter were stairs bordered by a dark wood banister that went to the second floor. There were two red padded chairs near the window with the frilly curtains that Zack could see now were badly faded. Salmon colored wallpaper enveloped the entire room. The monotony of it was broken by a painting of Custer's last stand. It depicted Custer bravely standing in the midst of massive carnage and taking careful aim with his pistol. For a moment, Zack was transported back to that day. It caused his heart to quicken. *That fool. Thank God I was with Reno*. He took a breath and exhaled. Beneath the painting was a pot-bellied stove, which was to the right of the chairs. In between the chairs and just under the window was a small table with an ashtray and several books on it. Directly in front of the table was a brass spittoon. To the left of the lobby was a small dining room with what appeared to be a cherry wood table and chairs for eight. Underlying both rooms was a powder blue carpet.

Zack stepped up to the counter. A wooden rack of cubby hole boxes hung on the wall behind it. All of the boxes but two had keys in them. Hanging on the wall next to this was a large Winchester Firearms calendar depicting a cowboy shooting a charging grizzly bear with a Winchester repeater. Beneath the colorful picture was a tear off page for the month of September 1883. Zack was about to ring the brass hand bell on the counter when an older, frumpy looking woman in a blue dress silently emerged from the hallway. She had salt and pepper hair that was coiled on the back of her head in a bun. Her gray eyes were bloodshot and tired looking. She said curtly, as if she was being inconvenienced, "Can I help you?"

Zack, who was carrying his rifle and nothing else, said, "Yes Ma'am, I need ah room for the night."

The woman sighed slightly and licked the edge of her mouth while she moved behind the counter. As she walked her heft caused her to sway from side to side. She turned the ledger so Zack could read it and shoved it towards him. "Room five up the stairs. That'll be a dollar or a dollar and ah half if you want breakfast."

Zack signed his name and pulled two dollars from his pocket. He set the money on the counter. "Any chance a fella could git something ta eat tonight?"

The woman picked up the money without looking at Zack. "This ain't a restaurant. I only cook for guests, breakfast and dinner."

"Well, I'm a guest."

"You weren't when supper was served."

"So, I couldn't talk ya out of a piece pie and a cup ah coffee?

The woman frowned as she made change from a drawer beneath the counter and handed it and a room key to Zack. She then allowed her eyes to meet his. She said with enough indifference in her voice to settle the matter but not so much to lose him as a customer, "You might go down to China-town, that is if ya like that kinda food. Personally, I don't care for it but you won't find anything else open this time of night."

For a brief moment, Zack made eye contact with the woman so that she would know what he thought of her lack of hospitality. But if it mattered to her, it didn't show. He turned to leave.

"Breakfast is from six to seven. Don't be late if ya wanna eat."

Zack smiled disingenuously towards the woman. "Yes Ma'am."

Before going in search of something to eat, Zack went upstairs and dropped his rifle off. His room was better than he expected. It had a bed, chair near the window, small dresser with a mirror above it, a wash basin with a pitcher of water and a chamber pot. A mostly green and yellow flowery wallpaper covered the walls except where a small painting of some snow-capped mountains was hanging. He was tempted to just go to bed, but he did not.

Silence met Zack as he stepped out onto the hotel's front porch. The old man in the rocking chair had gone off some-where. *Probably went to relieve himself*, thought Zack. He smiled, recalling the stranger's warning about the woman inside and how true it proved to be. As he stepped down from the porch, he was still undecided if he wanted to search out something to eat in Chinatown or just have a stiff drink and go to bed. Eating won out. There seemed to be fewer lights showing now and no one on the street. Having lived in the Boise Basin but three years, he could count on one hand the number of times that he'd been to Idaho City as Pla-cerville generally provided him with all that he ever needed. He shook his head and said to himself as he started walking towards where he believed Chinatown to be, *Well, this 'll be interestin'*. He went by a bank, a couple of vacant buildings, an American café, that according to the sign in the window had closed two hours ago, and a general store without seeing a single person. And then just ahead, a man stepped out from an older looking log building. The red letters on the sign above its door were peeling badly making it difficult to read that it was the, OWL BAR. The stranger glanced in Zack's direction and then turned away and started walking.

A sudden impulse of doubt caused Zack to call out, "Sir, excuse me."

The stranger, a man of medium build dressed as a miner, stopped and turned around. He said simply with a hint of caution in his voice, "Yes."

Zack stopped about five feet from the man. "Can you tell me where there might be a good place ta eat in Chinatown?"

The man, who appeared to be about 40 years old, had a thick black moustache. He was wearing a flat cap and his heavy canvas pants were caked with mud up to the knees. His response was immediate, he laughed and then said, "What the hell do ya wanna go over there an' eat for? All yer gonna git is either rice and pork or rice and fish."

The tenderness in his side from where he'd been shot coupled with his overall fatigue washed over Zack. He came back, "Well sir, it's been a long day and right now I ain't too particular about the chuck I eat."

The stranger hesitated for a moment as if he was trying to guess the circumstances that had put Zack in this situation, but then he let go of it. He pointed across the street and down it to where a side street came in. "Over there is Chinatown proper but hell, there's more Chinese here now than there is white folks. Purty soon it'll all be Chinatown."

Zack looked to where the stranger was pointing. "What's the name of this eatin' place?"

"Café."

"That's it, Café."

"They got a bunch of Chinese chicken scratches below that but I ain't never know'd what they meant. You can't miss it. Fair sized red sign with big yellow letters."

"You reckon they're still open?"

"Don't know. I ain't been there but once and that was right about usual supper time."

It occurred to Zack that maybe the stranger wasn't the authority he thought he was on what there was to eat at the Café since he'd only been there once, but he did not question it. "Much obliged, Mister."

Zack had already started across Main Street when the stranger called out, "Enjoy yer rice." And then he laughed.

Zack kept on walking. Within a couple of minutes he came to the side street where the stranger had said to go. It didn't look much different than Main Street other than there was more Chinese writing and fancy animal caricatures on signs and windows. And one other difference, there were no vacant buildings. The Café's sign was as the man had said it would be. Zack stopped in front of a little lavender colored building with a tin stovepipe protruding from its tarpapered roof. Dark blue smoke was rolling out of the stovepipe like the fire had just been tended. A small four pane window to the right of the door revealed light and movement inside. It had occurred to Zack that he might not be welcome given the way white people treated the Chinese, but he was here. And then he smiled as he said to himself, *Hell, how bad can it be. I already been shot today.* And with that he stepped inside.

It was a small room which made it all the more natural for people to turn to see who had come in. The tiny space was immediately smothered in silence save for the sizzling of something cooking on the stove. There were three customers and the cook, who was behind a half wall that defined the kitchen at the back of the room. All of them were staring at Zack. A subdued hostility permeated the air. Had he not been a white guy he figured they would've gone back to eating and talking by now, but they did not. He made eye contact with the cook as if to request permission to stay but the cook stood still, his expression did not change. Zack snorted so as to be barely audible and tossed his head slightly. *Well, the hell with 'em then*, he said to himself. He'd about reached the door when a voice behind him called out, "Mister, you want eat?"

It flashed in Zack's mind to keep on going but for some reason he stopped, curious as to why the cook had changed his mind. He turned and faced the man. The anger in his eyes had mostly hid itself. Zack said, trying to keep the edge from his voice, "Yes sir, I do." And then he added, trying to be cordial, "I'm a good ways the other side ah gant."

The cook, a little man with a wispy moustache and a black skull cap that covered the origin of a long black braid of hair that hung down the man's back, smiled weakly, obviously not understanding Zack's reference to being really hungry. He pointed to the only empty table. "Please sit."

Zack took a seat at the table the cook had pointed to. Its surface was barren of anything, not even a tablecloth. Before he could ask for a menu, the cook came back, "It late. You like chop suey, fried rice. Nothing else."

Zack could feel the other customer's eyes upon him, waiting to see what he would say. They were all Chinese men, two at one table and one at the only remaining table in the place. Their attire was similar, quilted jackets and duck cloth pants that were soiled to the knees and black slouch hats that were irregularly shaped. They remained quiet, as if Zack's presence had rendered them mute. Tilting his head back so he could see out from beneath the rim of his hat and make eye contact with the cook, Zack said, even though he had no idea what chop suey was, "That'll do." And then he added, "I'll take a cup of yer coffee too."

The cook shook his head. "No coffee, only tea."

The naysayer in Zack's mind instantly shouted out, *Well, what the hell kinda joint is this that don't have coffee. I don't remember the last time I took supper without it.* But then it occurred to him that the town was mostly Chinese and that it only made sense for the cook to serve what they liked. He said, grinning, "Well sir, I reckon it'll be tea then."

The cook nodded without saying anything else and went back to the kitchen. To Zack's right, barely ten feet away along the opposite wall, the other patrons had gone back to eating with an occasional glance in his direction. Zack suspected he was still the object of their attention as their voices sounded angry at times. It made him feel uneasy and he was regretting having come there, but then his stomach growling coupled with the nagging pain in his side from where he'd been shot countered his uneasiness. He said to himself, *I'll git something hot ta eat and go ta bed. That otta put me on the mend.* He removed his hat and set it on the table off to his left. He then ran his fingers through his hair in a gesture of fatigue as he looked down and yawned. The day's events were catching up to him.

"Here your tea."

Zack jerked back to allow the cook to set a little white tea pot with a tiny cup on the table. "Much obliged."

Once again, the cook nodded and went away without saying anything else.

Zack poured himself some tea. He wanted to laugh at the size of the cup but knew better. He took a noisy sip. *Hell, this ain't much better 'n hot water.* But it made him feel good inside. He took another sip and another until he had finished the cup without setting it down. From the corner of his eye he could see that he had attracted the attention of his friends across the room. Nonetheless, he poured himself another, cup as he did he noticed on the wall above the men a sign that read, SAM WO – PROPRIETOR. It was situated in between a fancy red paper fan that was open and affixed to the wall and a painting of a temple in a place that Zack supposed was China. He speculated too, that Sam Wo was the cook as he allowed his eyes to rove around the room while sipping more tea. All of it, including the rough plank floor, appeared to have been made from the Ponderosa pine trees that no longer existed on the mountains surrounding town. Even the tables and chairs were made from the trees dubbed 'yellow pine'. On the wall above Zack was a Chinese calendar. It had a picture of a pretty Chinese woman in a forest setting. He was looking up at it when the cook arrived with two steaming bowls. Zack looked at the food. The rice bowl had a spoon in it and the chop suey a fork. "You ok now?" asked the cook.

Zack nodded. "Believe I am." He then reached for his fork with the intention of starting to eat when it became obvious that the cook wasn't going away.

The cook said, stating what Zack figured was the obvious, "You no miner. You cowboy?"

Zack laughed. "Yeah, I ain't never been one that likes diggin' rocks."

And then like a highly charged bolt of lightning, the cook came back, "You know where Elk Meadow?"

Zack set his fork back in the bowl. Even though they hadn't spoken a word of English, the other three Chinamen across the room were now locked onto him. He looked hard at the cook. "Why do you ask?"

"I hear story Chinese man get killed there. I may want go there one day soon."

"You know Toby Sing?"

The cook nodded. "He come here lot."

There was little doubt in Zack's mind who told the cook about what took place at Elk Meadows but he asked anyway, "Who told you about Toby?"

The cook immediately looked fearful. "A friend."

"Li Ming? Did she tell you?"

"No, no. She no tell."

Zack moved on. "Why do you want to go there? It's a long ways and the country gits rough."

Anguish overtook the cook's face. "Friend tell me Toby Sing no get bury. Just leave for animals. I want gather his bones. Send home."

Zack had heard that most Chinese who had come to America didn't want to be buried here, at least not permanently they didn't. Their custom, or so he'd been told, was after several years in the ground the body would be dug up, the bones cleaned and placed in a small metal box that was shipped back to where they had come from in China. He said, "Toby got buried."

The cook's face showed disbelief that was fading towards hopefulness. Still, he came back, "My friend say Toby no bury. Say big black birds all over him."

"For a time they were, but then after Bickers left, my friend and I buried Toby."

The cook looked surprised. "Why you do?"

"It was the right thing to do."

"You one of the men my friend say try to help. Why you want to help Chinese man, Chinese woman. Bickers very bad man."

Zack glanced over the cook's shoulder at the other three Chinamen across the room who were all turned in their chairs and listening. The hatefulness that had radiated from their eyes just a few minutes ago was now gone. *Purty damned sad these people can't understand why ah white man would want ta help 'em*, said Zack to himself. He began to feel uneasy with the cook's praise. He said, hoping to end the conversation, "I don't know that I helped matters much."

"You try, that what count."

Zack looked the cook in the eye. "Thank you." And then he extended his hand. "Name's Zack Kotter."

Surprise came to the cook's face causing him to hesitate before shaking Zack's hand. "My name Sam Wo."

"Pleased ta meet ya," said Zack with a smile.

Sam's demeanor remained serious. He looked uncertain if he should say what was clearly in his mind but then he put it out there, almost like the words had escaped, "Someday you show Sam where Toby Sing buried?"

Zack nodded. "Yeah, I can do that."

Sam smiled and bowed just slightly towards Zack. "I be much obliged."

In his mind Zack could see Elk Meadows and all that had happened there. The images flashed in his mind like cloud to cloud lightning. There'd not been an hour go by since then that he hadn't seen something from the meadow, but mostly it was Li Ming's bloodied face. It caused him to ask, "How is it that Li Ming came to be at the Ore Chute?"

The newfound calm in Sam's face suddenly went away. He looked as if he had been betrayed but then he said, in a serious but matter of fact tone, "Li Ming's father very poor. He sell her to bad people. They sell her to Bickers. She owe him much money."

Zack shook his head. *How in the hell could a father do that*? He said aloud, "So she's workin' off her debt?"

Sam nodded. "Yes, she long time to go."

Zack had told himself that it was foolish thinking to have an interest in a whore, that there would be no good come of it, but she kept showing up in his mind. He sighed as he reached for his fork. "She's in a bad spot."

CHAPTER SEVEN

It was, he knew, in recognition of what he and Able had done at Elk Meadows that Sam Wo refused to accept Zack's money for what he had eaten. The meal had set well with him in spite of what he'd been told about the food at the Café. Lights were fewer now as the night had progressed. At the intersection with Main Street, Zack could see further to the west several horses tied out front of what he was fairly certain was the Ore Chute Saloon and sporting house. He'd been tired before he'd eaten his fill of chop suey and rice but now, he was even more so. Common sense told him he should go back to his room and get some rest, but Li Ming was persistent in his mind. He began walking in that direction. It was as if he couldn't help himself. *No good 'll come of this. Bickers 'll be hopping mad ta see me in his establishment.* And then he was there, standing in front of the weathered two-story log building. There was light coming from a window upstairs that overlooked the street. An image of Li Ming being in that room doing what she did came to his mind. He sighed and started for the entrance. The upper third of the door was glass. As Zack reached for the brass knob, the naysayer in his mind was shouting out, *just go ta bed.* But through the glass, he could see her, sitting at a table with three white men, drinking. The men were loud and boisterous. Suddenly, the man sitting closest to Li Ming, a big man, pulled her from her chair and onto his lap. He began groping her and laughing and nuzzling his coal black beard into her chest. Li Ming angrily pushed back from the man. She said something that Zack could not hear that made the bearded man laugh in mock fear.

Zack twisted the knob and pushed the door open. There was a steady drone of voices punctuated occasionally by a loud laugh or obscenity coming from the half dozen or so tables with chairs to the right of the bar. A blue haze of tobacco smoke hung over the room. It swirled in the yellow light coming from several lanterns hanging from the ceiling. A moth trying desperately to extend its life before the onset of fall fluttered vainly around the lantern at the rear of the room. The poker players at the table beneath it seemed unconcerned with its plight. No one, not even Li Ming, took note of Zack's entrance as he walked over to the bar on the left side of the room. A little skinny man in a white shirt with a black bow tie and a black vest greeted him. "What 'll be Mister?"

"Believe I'll have a coupla fingers of Old Grandad if ya got it."

The bartender nodded and turned away, as he did Zack eyed him, with his short black hair and neatly trimmed moustache. He didn't seem to fit the image of the sort of man that Zack had envisioned working for Bickers. He watched as the wispy little man plucked the bottle of Old Grandad from the many liquor bottles resting on the back bar beneath the mirror on the wall. The little man took a short glass from those stacked in front of the bottles and set it down right side up. He made a generous pour. Momentarily, he appeared before Zack and set the drink on the bar. "That 'll be two-bits."

Zack fished a quarter out of his pocket and dropped it in the bartender's hand. The little man turned away without speaking but before he could go Zack came back, as if he didn't know who Li Ming was, "How much would a roll in the hay with that little China girl over there cost a fella?"

"Three dollars," said the bartender in a tone that suggested it was common knowledge.

Zack feigned insult. "Holy shit, that little girl is purty proud ah herself."

"She don't set the price."

Zack laughed sarcastically. "She probably don't git ta keep much ah that three dollars either, I bet."

The little man frowned and walked away.

Zack took a sip of his whiskey, as he did he surveyed the room in the mirror behind the bar. There were animal heads on the wall behind him. A mule deer, mountain goat, elk and a black bear rug all dull and dirty looking from years of smoke and dust. The ceiling seemed low but that was because there was a second story with rooms for prostitutes and Bickers. A hallway at the far end of the room led to the stairs at the back of the building. On the wall to the right of the stairs, just across from the poker table, was a painting of a nude woman lying on her side. She was plump, and to Zack's way of thinking, *not all that purty*. There were about a dozen patrons, mostly white men, and three saloon girls working the tables. Wooden stools lined the front of the bar, only one of them, about midway between Zack and the bartender who'd gone to the opposite end of the bar, was occupied. Overall, the room had a shadowy appearance.

Zack took another sip of his whiskey, keeping his eyes straight ahead into the mirror and the table where Li Ming was at. *She don't recognize me*, he said to himself. He sighed. *It was some distance. Maybe all cowboys look alike to her.* And then he snorted. *Well, what if she does recognize you mister knight in shining armor? What then? She's stuck here, ya damned fool.* And then the naysayer in Zack came down hard on him. *Just what the hell are you doing here anyway, eyeing a whore from afar like some lovestruck schoolboy?*

She's Bickers' property. Hell, she's anybody's property that's got three dollars. You need ta just git outta here. Ain't no good gonna come of this. He had been leaning against the bar, but Zack now stood up and slightly away from it as he made a deliberate effort to finish his drink. He set the empty glass on the bar and started to turn away when he saw that Li Ming was looking in his direction. Her focus was more down than up. Zack looked at his stovepipe boots and the fact he was generally the exception in tucking his pants into the tops of them.

Suddenly, Li Ming wriggled free from the big miner and started towards Zack. Her eyes were now fixed on his. She stopped within a few feet of him. She looked again at his boots and then up at Zack. Her voice was hopeful, "You cowboy at Elk Meadows?"

She was a good head shorter than Zack. He looked down at her. Tears had already begun to form in her black eyes. He said simply, "I am."

"I grateful for what you try to do. It mean much to me."

"I'm just sorry we couldn't git ya free ah those scoundrels. It ain't right the way they were treatin' ya."

Tears were trickling down Li Ming's cheeks. "But you try, that what matters. No one ever do that for Li Ming."

And then the light from the lantern just beyond Li Ming was interrupted by the big miner on whose lap she had been sitting. He grabbed Li Ming by the arm and pulled her back. She tried to break free but he wouldn't allow it. He said, in a loud voice that was dripping with anger, "Me an' this China gal was about to conduct some business so I'd be obliged Mister if you just went on yer way."

From the corner of his eye, Zack saw the bartender heading down the hallway that led upstairs and likely where Bickers was and that everyone in the room was looking at him. He became aware too that the din of noise in the room had died away. There was a palpable expectation of what was about to happen. The naysayer in his mind was screaming at him to not say it but the words came out as if they were as mandatory as breathing, "Friend, me an' the lady was talkin' so I'd be obliged if you'd unhand her."

The big man tossed his head back and laughed sarcastically. "Lady, there ain't no *ladies* in this place and I ain't yer friend, you simple ass cow herder."

Zack took a step towards the big man causing Li Ming to cry out, "It ok, I go with him." But it was too late. The big man flung her to the side and lunged at Zack driving him back into the heavy oak bar. The impact knocked the wind out of Zack and for a moment left him defenseless, enabling the big man to land a good punch to his face. But then the immense amount of adrenaline in his system allowed him to come back with a hard right of his own to the stranger's gut and then a left to the other side of his belly and finally a right in the center of his face, crushing his nose and creating a free-flowing stream of blood over his lips and into his dark beard. The big man was staggered by the body blows and perhaps shocked by the blood that came away from having put his hands to his face. He was wobbly, barely standing, when beyond him Zack could see the big man's friends shoving their chairs back and start toward him. And then he saw Li Ming, still on the floor, point with a terrified look on her face. He started to turn and then everything went black.

Bickers stood over Zack, still holding the pistol with which he'd cold-cocked him. His look was haughty and mean. "Get up you sorry sonovabitch."

Zack emitted a low moan as his senses started to come back.

"C'mon get up, mister tough cowboy."

Zack slowly gathered his hands to where he could push himself up from the dirty wood floor. The pain in his head was excruciating. It caused him to not want to open his eyes, but he knew to linger where he was at would not bode well for him. He'd just gotten to his hands and knees when Bickers took a step towards him, as if to generate momentum, and kicked him in the gut. The blow knocked the wind out of Zack. It caused him to hunch up like he'd been gut shot. For a moment, he was frozen in that position with his head resting on the floor fighting to catch his breath. Bickers was poised to deliver another kick when Li Ming, who had gotten to her feet, suddenly rushed him and started flailing at him with her fists while screaming, "Stop it, stop it."

An angry rage consumed Bickers' face. "Why you little bitch. Strike me will ya." And then, like he was swatting a fly, he back-handed Li Ming hard sending her to the floor beside Zack. She began to sob uncontrollably, blood oozing from a new cut on her bottom lip.

Zack twisted his head to where he could make eye contact with Li Ming. She was near hysterical. The look in her eyes was one of terror and hopelessness. It was a look that he'd seen before in the faces of men about to die.

And then Bickers yelled over his shoulder. "Ed, take this ungrateful whore to her room and lock her in it."

Bickers' lackey stepped around him and reached down, grabbed Li Ming by the hair and jerked her to her feet. Li Ming began to wail, "No, no, let go of me." But it was to no avail as Ed's grip on her long hair was tight, bending her head in the direction he wanted to go. She had no choice but to trail after him, half stumbling and walking and crying all the way back to the hallway. And then her cries and sobs had an echo to them until they finally went away.

Enraged, Zack got partially to his feet and lunged towards Bickers. Sensing that it was coming, Bickers stepped back and fired his pistol into the floor just in front of Zack's head. The report of the gun was deafening in the confined space of the bar room. It stopped Zack as quick as if he'd been shot in the brain. Bickers shouted, "You damned fool. You try that again and I'll put some hot lead in ya."

Zack struggled to stand up. His gunshot wound from that morning had begun to bleed again. It had soaked through his shirt, but he was oblivious to it while breathing heavily and staring hatefully at Bickers. "You'll git yer place in hell one day. Men like you always do."

Bickers scoffed. "Well, if I do you won't have anything to do with it. Now get outta my place 'fore I change my mind about shootin' you right here and now."

Zack bent over and picked up his hat. He grimaced as he put it on over the bump that had risen on the back of his head where he had been hit. He looked one last time at Bickers and shook his head as if the very sight of him was disgusting.

Bickers came back, "Don't prod me, cowboy."

Zack smiled sarcastically. "We'll have this dance again someday. You can rest assured when we do, I'll be leadin'." And with that Zack started for the door. His expectation of being shot was so great that by the time he reached the door the muscles in his back had tensed up, as if they could deflect a bullet, to the point they were hurting.

It was not a good night. There had been more than ample time for Zack to second guess his decision to go to the Ore Chute as sleep had been hard to come by. His head throbbed, thanks to Bickers, and his side was painful too, even though the bleeding had stopped. At breakfast it had been just him and the old man on the porch from last night and Mrs. Hays, the grumpy woman who owned the hotel. The old man of course wanted to know how it was that Zack came to have blood on his shirt. The necessity of having to tell the story lest he be perceived as rude caused Zack to eat faster in order to escape the grilling of the stranger. Needless to say, his stay at the hotel had been anything but restful.

With the dawning of a new day the town had come to life. Businesses were open and people were on the street, Zack being one of them. At half past eight he was about a hundred yards from the jail when he observed a neatly dressed man in a dark suit coat that was open revealing a black vest and white shirt, and occasionally, a glimpse of a badge. The man had just left the sheriff's office and was headed towards Zack. It appeared this was by coincidence until, when he was about 30 feet away, he spied the blood on Zack's shirt. His dark eyes then locked onto Zack's, leaving no doubt as to his destination. When they had gotten to within normal conversation distance it was obvious to Zack that the sheriff recognized him but his look was peculiar, maybe bordering on perturbed. It gave Zack an uneasy feeling that suddenly became justified. "So, yer the fella causing the ruckus down at the Ore Chute last night."

Zack was taken aback to the point it allowed the sheriff time to sling another arrow his way. "I've little patience for a man causing trouble over a whore."

Zack was still processing how it was that Sheriff Snyder had come by this information so early in the day when he spit the words out, "Seven o'clock in the damned morning and I got Hyrum Bickers in my office ah chewing on my ear. I'll tell ya, cowboy, I don't need that kind ah aggravation that early."

Zack glared at Snyder. His appearance with his nice clothes, near new black Stetson with its perfectly flat brim, and his neatly trimmed moustache suggested life was good for him. Even his sidearm, a Smith & Wesson, double action .44 Caliber that rode high in its holster on his right hip seemed better than what the average man would carry. *If he's friends with Bickers*, said Zack to himself, *I'll probably be rockin' his boat in a big way*. He came back, "You should know, Sheriff, that business last night wasn't all my doing. A ruffian down there was treatin' one ah the ladies harshly."

The sheriff snorted and then laughed. "You do understand what those, *ladies*, do for a livin' don't ya?"

"Ain't no cause for a man ta treat 'em that way."

Snyder's look became stern, almost threatening, as he stared into Zack's eyes. He said, "Bickers told me about the trouble he had up in Elk Meadows. Said a Chinaman that took one of his girls drew on him and he had to shoot him. I talked to his boys and they back up how Bickers said it happened."

Zack laughed. The words come to his mind so quick that he couldn't contain them. "It'd take a real huckleberry ta believe those two."

The sheriff hesitated just long enough before responding that Zack knew the sheriff didn't believe Bickers either, but he came back, "You need to remember who you're talkin' to."

Zack feigned a look of contrition but did not verbalize it. Instead, he took a humble, almost pleading tone as he said, "Sheriff, Bickers shot Toby Sing in cold blood and his men beat Li Ming."

Snyder was un-moved. "The way I heard it is, that China-man had a gun. By law they aren't allowed to even own a fire-arm. So, he broke the law right there. Bickers said this Sing fella went for his pistol, so he had no choice but to shoot him. It's your word against his." Snyder paused as if he needed extra time to consider Li Ming's plight and then he said, "Bickers bought Li Ming. He's got a signed contract. She still owes him over a thousand dollars. I seen the paperwok."

Zack knew there was some truth to what the sheriff was saying as he'd heard that Chinese families, in times of need, would sometimes sell their daughters to work as servants or sometimes prostitutes. He said, haltingly, "Well, it still don't give Bickers the right to beat her."

The sheriff sighed and shook his head. "You know, with these laws that the government has got now, this Chinese Exclusion Act and the Page Act, I'd say it's a blessing that this Sing fella or Li Ming is even in this country."

Zack knew of the laws that forbid Chinese from coming to America but he came back, "Ain't no blessing ta git murdered or beaten."

Snyder frowned. "My deputy tells me that you and Harley O'Keefe were bushwhacked yesterday. Said Harley was killed. You got any idea who done it?"

Zack shook his head. "Harley had a run-in with some fellas he caught stealing his horses. They traded shots. Harley said he hit one of 'em but he wasn't certain how bad."

"Where was it that this took place?"

"Somewhere's down along the South Fork of the Payette."

Snyder tossed his head slightly. "That's way hell and gone up there. I don't get out that way much unless I got good reason."

"I guess you got reason now."

"Well, this is the first I heard of it."

Zack struggled to keep his face respectful. *Harley probably figured it wasn't worth the ride in here.* He said aloud, "It just happened a coupla days ago. You should know that Harley said one of these rustlers was ridin' a gray horse."

A weak smile came to Snyder's face. "I probably see a gray horse just about every day."

A pulse of anger surged through Zack. He purposely allowed it to flood his eyes. He came back. "Well, how often do you see a man carrying a .44-100 rifle?"

"Can't say as I've ever heard of it."

"One of the scalawags that bushwhacked me and Harley was shootin' that kind a gun. It was probably that fella that killed Harley, as it was a long shot."

"Where was it that this happened?

"Coupla miles east ah Harley's place on the road ta Placerville."

The sheriff sighed. "Well, I'll look into it but probably ain't much a fella can do now but keep an eye out for gray horses and this oddball gun."

There was something about the sheriff's tone that didn't set right with Zack. It caused him to come back with some edge in his voice, "I can take ya to this spot today. Soon as I fetch my horse from the livery, I'll be headed that way."

"To what end, Mr. Kotter?" said Snyder defensively. "You seem to have told me what there is to know about any likely shooter in this matter. You can be assured that I will remain vigilant to persons meeting these criteria and will take the appropriate action should I encounter them. But you should know too that I can't arrest a man simply because he rides a gray horse or possesses a .44-100 rifle."

It occurred to Zack that maybe the sheriff was right but, in that same instant, the scavenged, putrid smelling body of Toby Sing came to mind. He and Able had seen Toby get shot, *that should be proof enough*, he said to himself. He said aloud, "And Bickers shootin' that Chinaman in Elk Meadows?"

Anger flared in Snyder's eyes. "I already told you. It's his word against yours and he's got two witnesses that says this Chinaman went for his gun. Besides, there ain't no jury in these parts that's gonna convict a white man for shootin' a Chinaman."

Zack knew that Snyder was likely correct, still, he couldn't help himself, "Alright Sheriff, but this ain't right."

Snyder sighed heavily as if he was exasperated with the matter. He came back, "There's lots a things in life that ain't right. I reckon you can add this to your list. Good day, Mr. Kotter." And with that, Sheriff Snyder walked away.

For a brief moment, Zack watched Snyder as he went down the street greeting one person and another, doffing his hat to a woman and calling out a cheery, "Good morning, Ma'am" and then stopping to exchange pleasantries with a priest. Zack turned away and started toward the livery. He said to himself, *that fella knows where his bread is buttered and he ain't gonna do nuthin' to spoil it.* Zack's head throbbed with pain. He quickened his pace. *I just need ta git the hell outta this town. Shudda never come.*

He had just finished saddling Biscuits in the alleyway that ran between the stalls on either side of the livery stable when he heard someone behind him. Zack turned. The morning sun was pouring through the big open doors at the far end of the building. It was a situation of where the man coming towards Zack could see him clearly, while Zack was mostly blinded. He was struggling to see through the fine dust that roiled in the bright light when a voice came from it, "Mr. Kotter, it me, Sam Wo."

Surprised, Zack came back a little uncertain, "Sam – Good mornin' to ya. You headed outta town?"

Sam shook his head. "No," he said as he extended his hand towards Zack with a folded piece of paper. "I bring message from Li Ming."

"Li Ming? I didn't figure Bickers would let her leave the Ore Chute after all that's happened."

"You right. She not come. White girl bring paper. Say Li Ming locked up."

Zack unfolded the paper. It appeared to be a map drawn in pencil. There were several quivery lines that ran from the edge of a series of interconnected teeth or teepees that formed an oval. The shorter lines ran to one longer line that ran nearly the entire length of the oval. On one of the shorter lines, near where it attached to the teepees, was an x. But nowhere on the drawing was there a single word, not even in Chinese. It begged the question, "What is this?" asked Zack.

"White girl say this where Toby at."

Zack's face showed confusion. He said solemnly, "I don't need a map for that, Sam."

Sam allowed quiet to engulf them. He lowered his voice to a whisper. "We alone?"

"I think so. The liveryman was outside in the corral."

Sam stepped closer to Zack and then motioned for him to bend his head within whisper range. He said, "This map where Toby Sing find gold. He and Li Ming go there to dig for it when he killed."

Zack kept quiet and looked at the drawing again. It made sense to him now. He recalled how the main creek ran the length of Elk Meadows with tiny little tributaries coming down from springs that originated in the craggy rocks surrounding the basin. He pointed to the 'X' on the map. "There?"

"Yes."

Zack looked around and into the bright light and then, hearing the liveryman's voice outside, he whispered, "why is Li Ming giving me this?"

"Chinaman can't file on new claim. Only have old claim, already most gold gone. White man no want anymore. This new claim. Li Ming say you good man. You file on claim. All she ask you make enough money buy her freedom."

It was making sense to Zack now. Toby and Li Ming had gone to Elk Meadows to work this claim on the sly as neither, according to the law, could file on it. Misgivings about what he might be getting himself into were running rampant in his mind. At times he wondered if Li Ming wasn't such a pretty girl, if he would've gone to the Ore Chute last night. But it was too late to second guess that decision. He said, as if to forewarn Sam Wo and Li Ming, "I don't know spit about mining."

Sam smiled. "You learn. Li Ming count on you."

Zack sighed heavily, allowing the uncertainty to command his face. "I hear she owes Bickers over a thousand dollars, is that true?"

Embarrassed, Sam looked down staying quiet for a moment before raising his head. "It true. She owe eleven hundred fifty dollar,"

Zack shook his head. "That's a lotta gold."

"She never get ahead. Bickers, he take most what she earn. He bad man. Cheat Li Ming."

"It's gonna take time, so tell Li Ming to be patient." He paused and then added, "Tell her I won't be back until I have the money."

Sam smiled. "She be happy hear this. Be like light end of tunnel."

Zack nodded. "I hope it is."

CHAPTER EIGHT

It occurred to Zack that the solitude on the ride back from Idaho City to Placerville might not be a good thing. It gave him time, too much time, to think as Biscuits plodded along through the densely wooded mountains. *It's gonna be hurtful to Katherine when she learns of what I'm doin' for Li Ming,* he said to himself. *Folks ain't gonna understand me throwin' in with a prostitute. Katherine will be first in that line and right behind her will be Able and Shorty.* But then it came to him, *if I make this about the gold people will understand that. They'll think that is ok. People understand money.* He rode on, his mind temporarily cleansed of frustration, content to allow the birds and squirrels and the moan of the wind in the tops of the big pine trees to assuage his senses. For a while, these qualities and the warm fall sun made it a poor man's utopia, but then, just like that it exploded with the intensity of an artillery shell.

"Well, I'll be go ta hell," whispered Zack. "There's that sonovabuck now."

Up ahead coming around a blind curve in the road was a rider on a gray horse. Zack's heart had instantly begun to hammer away as if it was desperate to escape his chest. The rider did not look like a gun hand, at least he did not fit the image Zack had always held. Instead, the man, who appeared to be middle-aged, with short dark hair and moustache, was plainly dressed. He was wearing a dirty gray Stetson hat whose crown was dimpled on all sides. The brim on the left side was curled up slightly while the brim on the right side was flat with a slight tear in it. His shirt was an off-white color with vertical red stripes that were badly faded, over it, he wore a black vest that was buttoned up. Around his neck was a large red neckerchief. Black suspenders held up his dark brown cotton pants. He was well armed with what appeared to be an Army Colt .45 on his right hip and the stock of a rifle pointing forward from a scabbard on the right side of his horse. He was about 30 feet from Zack when he called out, "Mornin, friend."

Zack's mind was spinning like a windmill on a windy day. *I could just throw down on him right now, he won't be expectin' it. I'll march this sorry cuss back to Idaho City.* But then, the naysayer in his mind appealed to his common sense, *Snyder said he can't just arrest a man for riding a gray horse.* He knew the sheriff was right. Nonetheless, his reckless side was badgering him to draw on the stranger right up to the point of him shouting back, "Mornin to ya. Name's Zack Kotter. How ya fairin' ta-day?"

The stranger's expression did not change as he came back, "Well sir, I'm still on the right side ah the dirt so I reckon I'm fairin' ok. And you Sir, does this day suit ya?"

Zack was not oblivious to the fact the stranger had not given his name. He turned his head and spit a stream of tobacco juice off the right side of Biscuits. In the instant he loaded the words on his tongue to respond he could see that the stranger's eyes had settled on his bloodstained shirt. He said anyway, "Doing just fine."

The stranger nodded towards Zack's shirt. "It don't look it."

Zack glanced down at his shirt and then back at the man who he suspected might have been responsible for his wound. He locked eyes with the stranger and then said, allowing his words to be cold, "Some bushwhackin' sonovabitch shot me and a friend a couple days back. Killed my friend." Zack watched for a change in the man's expression. He had just insulted him, if he was the shooter.

If the stranger's face gave him away, it would be due to the fact he didn't show any emotion at all. He came back, his tone disingenuous, "That's too bad. I guess a fella can't never let his guard down."

"Kinda tough to guard against somebody shootin' ya from a good hide. Why hell, there could be somebody right now, out here in all these trees with a bead on one or the other of us. So, you tell me, how do you guard against that?"

The stranger jerked his head to the side as if to accentuate what he was about to say, "Well, I reckon you don't want ta git on anybody's bad side."

A pulse of anger shot through Zack. "It ain't that simple. I'm of the opinion the scoundrels that shot me and my neighbor is the same ones that's been stealing our stock. We got a right ta be mad. If anybody deserves bushwhackin' it's those thieving sons ah bitches."

The stranger cracked a smile. "Those fellas got ya purty riled up, have they?"

Zack immediately felt it, a knowingness between them as to how things really were. It was almost like the stranger was taunting him. He said, "Kinda makes a man want to turn the tables on these boys."

"You mean to bushwhack 'em?"

Zack looked the stranger hard in the eyes. "No, that's the coward's way."

Anger enveloped the man's face but as quick as it had come, he pulled it back like the good poker player that he was. He said, "Well Mr. Kotter, I wish you luck in finding those thieves but I've got to be on my way."

"Safe travels to you, Mister -, I don't believe I caught yer name?" Zack watched the stranger's reaction for any hesitation. There was none.

"Name's Bob Smith. I'm a miner by trade. I'm hopin' to find work down around Idaho City."

Zack said to himself, *he's either a practiced liar or he's tellin' the truth.* He said aloud, "I don't believe there's much work to be had down there. The mines is purty well played out."

The stranger frowned. "I'd heard that. Heard the Chinese is about the only ones doing much work, but I'll go on to Nevada 'fore I work that cheap."

Zack noticed the man's hands. Their appearance caused him to doubt his suspicions. They were calloused and dirty looking. *Maybe he is a miner,* he said to himself. *But if he can't find work, maybe he's taken to rustling?* He turned his head to the side and spit again as a Steller's jay began screeching in a big ponderosa pine behind him. In his gut he wanted to believe that this was one of the shooters but, at the same time, the words of the sheriff echoed in his mind, *you can't arrest a man for riding a gray horse.* Frustrated, he said, "Good day to ya, Mr. Smith." Not waiting for a response, Zack nudged Biscuits' sides and started on down the road.

By the time he got to the general store in Placerville, it was early afternoon. It'd only been in the last little ways that he'd finally convinced himself that he needed to make a clean break with Katherine. There'd be no telling her about Li Ming or the gold claim he was supposed to locate so he could buy Li Ming's freedom. He'd just tell her that he didn't feel the same way about her as she did him. As he looked up from tying Biscuits to the hitching rail in front of the store, an older woman with gray hair in a lavender colored skirt and white blouse appeared in the doorway. She looked straight at Zack and smiled. "If you're looking for Katherine, she's gone to Harley O'Keefe's funeral. Her and her folks, they left before noon."

A surprised look came to Zack's face. "Oh, I was thinkin' they'd bury him tomorrow."

The woman's right hand was clutching a white handkerchief with little yellow flowers embroidered on it. She raised it to her chest and held it there like it served some purpose. "That friend of yours came to town late yesterday to get more nails for the coffin and to let folks know they were going to bury Mr. O'Keefe today."

Harley musta started ta ripen, said Zack to himself. To the woman on the porch, he said, "Did my friend state the time of the service?"

"About right now, two o'clock."

Zack grimaced. "I was hopin' ta make it to his burying."

The woman now took note of his blood-stained shirt. "My thoughts on the matter is you'd be better off going to see Doc Holten and get that wound tended to. You do that and hang around a little while, maybe Katherine will be back from the funeral." The old woman paused and smiled big. "You know she's real sweet on you. You know that, don't you"

Zack looked at the woman, a little taken aback. She stood there like she was waiting for him to express his feeling for Katherine, but he did not. A blend of guilt and shame flooded his mind, this along with the growing awkward silence between him and the old woman caused him to finally say, "I'd be obliged if you'd tell Katherine that I stopped by."

"You should just wait for her," said the woman in a louder voice as Zack got on Biscuits.

Zack looked at the woman and touched his right hand to the brim of his hat. "You have yerself ah good evening, Ma'am." And with that he started out of town. It was with some apprehension that he went on towards Harley's place. There would be nothing good there, not Harley's grieving widow and kids, nor a reckoning with Katherine, even riding past the blood soaked dirt in the road where Harley had bled out. Not a damned thing, but he knew they'd be expecting him.

The slit of road that snaked its way through the thick timber was in heavy shadow owing to the sun being nearly down and what was left of it being shrouded in black storm clouds. He was, he guessed, about five miles from Harley's place when, off to his left, he caught glimpses through the trees of a buggy coming at a good clip. With his eyes he followed its progress until the road curved back and the buggy and its two-horse team was coming straight at him. He reined Biscuits to the side of the road to allow the buggy to pass. In the distance he could hear the pop of the driver's whip and then, as the buggy drew near, he could see the horses flared nostrils, their heavy breathing and the sweaty lather on their chests. It was a long, steep pull from Harley's place to the divide that dropped down to Placerville. It was a good five miles. Anger surged within Zack. *That dumb sonovabitch is gonna kill those horses.* He'd just put out his hand to stop the driver when he suddenly realized who he was looking at. The driver flashed a perturbed scowl as he brought the team to a halt. His expression carried over to his words, "Mr. Kotter, I guess you realize I've lost my momentum going up this hill."

From the back seat came Katherine's voice, "Father –"

"Quiet, Katherine."

Zack stared hard at Katherine's father. He purposely coated his words with sarcasm, "Well Mr. Halsey, you keep driving these horses as hard as you are and you'll lose more than yer momentum."

Ephriam Halsey glared at Zack. "They're a good stout team. They're up to it. Besides, can't you see there's a storm coming."

"There ain't no call for it, Sir. You need ta pace these animals, from here to the divide. Stop every now and again, rest 'em. That's a steep sonovabuck. You otta know that."

Halsey scoffed. "I don't have the patience or time to sit here and be talked to like I'm some wet behind the ears kid by the likes of you." And with that Halsey snapped his whip over the backs of the horses, drowning out Katherine's sobs of, "I'm sorry, Zack. I'm sorry."

In the poor light, Zack made brief eye contact with Katherine as the buggy clattered off. It was a look tainted by his anger for her father. It caused him to barely raise his hand from the pommel of his saddle and then she was gone. He did not turn and watch them go up the mountain as a man might do if someone that he loved were in the buggy. And then came the pop of the whip and an indiscernible shout. Zack seethed the words, "That sorry cuss." The image of him catching up to the buggy and stopping it flashed in his mind. But it did not end there. Katherine's father was arrogant and hot-headed. A fight ensued. Katherine and her mother were crying and screaming. It would not be good. Zack sighed heavily, hoping to expel these thoughts from his mind. For a moment he sat there, as this kaleidoscope of angry emotion melted away until, finally, he nudged Biscuits and moved on.

By the time he reached the fork in the road that would either take him home or to Harley's place, a sprinkling of rain had started to fall. It was, not yet anyway, a rain that would make a man real wet. It was more annoying than anything. The dark clouds overhead had pulled a black curtain all the way across the sky so as to not allow for even a speck of what little sunlight remained to peak through. In Zack's mind his guilt, or sense of obligation to go pay his respects to Harley's widow, was wrestling with his common sense. *If I go there, I'll most likely be rolling my blankets out in the barn tonight*, he said to himself. And then he looked to his right and home. *Or, I sleep in my own bed.* He reckoned it was the evil in him that called to mind, *there'll likely be good eats at Harley's. Always is after a funeral.* Suddenly, his conscience jumped into the fray. *Zack Kotter, yer a downright shit for thinkin' such a thing when old Harley has just been put under today. What a shit you are. His family is likely beside themselves with sorrow and here you are thinkin' about eatin'.* But then the reality of the pain in his head and side and the burning in his gut from not having eaten since that morning surged to the forefront.

He sighed deeply, as if he could shed his pain and fatigue, and then he reined Biscuits towards Harley's. He continued at a slow pace trying to think of what to tell Mrs. O'Keefe of how Harley was that morning. Nothing special came to mind. The rain was still gentle but of big drops that caused the dust in the road to puff up when they landed leaving a little moist crater.

A well-worn set of wagon tracks cutoff from the main road that continued on down to the valley and the South Fork of the Payette. A strip of sagebrush and grass ran between where the wheels had ground away the vegetation to floury dirt. Zack had just turned onto these tracks when he met a man and a woman in a buggy headed out to the main road and home. The man, whom Zack recognized as someone that he'd met several months ago, waved but did not stop. There were Hereford cattle amongst the scattered ponderosa pine and yellow grass and gray sage to either side of the two-track. Most of the trees were no taller than about twelve feet, owing to the fact that a fire had gone through there not too many years ago. *These is some fine lookin' cattle*, said Zack to himself. *Harley's probably keepin' 'em close to the house on account of all the thievery going on.*

In about a half a mile the old burn gave way to mature ponderosa pine trees. Some of them would measure three feet across at the base and over a hundred feet tall. In places, their branches high above interlocked with one another making a canopy of sorts that blocked out even more of what little light remained in the day. *This is 'bout like ridin' into a mineshaft*, thought Zack. He rode on, maybe a quarter mile, when abruptly he came to a clearing where the big trees had been cut down to make room for Harley's log cabin, corrals, a garden and other out buildings. Yellow light showed in the house, which was straight ahead, and from the open doors of the barn off to his left. There were no horses or buggies near the house as he had envisioned, nor was there any wailing and crying. It was quiet, save for the crickets. Smoke drifted unsteadily up from the stovepipe on the roof suggesting to Zack that the fire needed tending. For the most part, it appeared like any other night, quiet and peaceful with Harley inside having a cup of coffee while his wife and daughter washed the supper dishes. But that illusion was shattered when Zack spied off to his right, just barely visible beyond the crumbling stalks of this past season's corn crop, a solitary grave with a wooden cross. A giant yellow pine stood guard over it. The grave brought back images of Harley lying dead on the road and, in the next instant, he was at their barn, laughing and talking with them, unaware that in a little while he would be dead. It caused Zack to shiver when he thought of how death could be right around the next bend in the trail. *It's good a man can't see into his future and know when his time is up*, he said to himself. And then his mind gave into it, that day on the Little Bighorn. *Those boys knew they was doomed. Only good part of it was they didn't have long to fret about it.* He sighed, trying to wash away the images of their mutilated bodies. He whispered, "I was so damned lucky ta be with Reno."

From the near darkness towards the barn came a voice, "Evenin' Mister. Somethin' I can do for ya?"

Zack looked over. A middle-aged man holding a milk bucket in his right hand stood in the doorway of the barn. Zack called out to the man as he started Biscuits in that direction. Me an' my partners got a place over on Quartz Crik. I just come by ta pay my respects."

The man, still holding the bucket of milk, came back, "I guess ya know you missed the service. We buried Harley this afternoon."

Zack reined Biscuits to a stop. He nodded in the direction of the grave. "I see that. Was it well attended?"

The man shrugged. "There was 15 or 20. I don't know. I didn't count. All I know is my back is aching from diggin' that grave and then fillin' it in. That's ah helluva lot ah dirt. You ever dug a grave, Mister?"

Zack didn't appreciate the man's irreverence but he didn't go there, he said simply, "I've had some experience in those matters."

"Well then, you know that what's on top of the ground ain't necessarily what a feller is going ta find when he gits down a foot or two. I'll tell ya this was ah cobbly sonvabitch. It ain't enough that I gotta dig postholes all day on this rock pile but I -" Suddenly, the man went quiet as he picked up on Zack's disapproving stare.

Zack stepped down from Biscuits. He said, "I take it you work for Harley?"

"Yeah, me and a friend hired on about a month ago. Been building fence mostly."

Zack studied the man's thin build, the salt and pepper stubble on his face and his dark eyes that seemed to have been placed deeper in their sockets than most people's. His gray cotton shirt that hung off of his bony shoulders only added to his unhealthy appearance. Zack came back, "Where is it you come from?"

Right away, the man's eyes became nervous. "Why is it yer askin?"

Zack laughed briefly so as to make the man look foolish for questioning his motive. He said, "Just trying ta be sociable, Mister. If it's a secret you can keep it to yerself."

The thin man set the bucket of milk on the ground. He then shook his arm a couple of times to rid himself of the cramp he'd developed as if this took priority over answering Zack's question. Finally, he said, "I hail from a lotta places. The last one being Nevada."

"You punchin' cattle down that way?"

Almost like it was a reflex, the hesitancy came back to the man's face but then he answered, lest he draw attention to it,

"No, I was workin' in the mines until they got all that cheap Chinese labor. It ain't no better here either."

Since he had no stake in the matter, Zack did not challenge the thin man's assertion of how things were. He moved on, "Be all right with you if I tend to my horse and turn him into yer pasture for tonight."

"Help yerself." And with that the thin man picked up the bucket of milk and started towards the house.

"Much obliged," said Zack in a louder voice. And then he called out to the thin man's back, "Tell Mrs. O'Keefe I'll be along just as soon as I tend to my horse."

The thin man did not respond but kept on in his lopsided hobble with the heavy milk bucket towards the house. *That fella is an unsociable cuss*, said Zack to himself. *He's tired and hurtin' but so am I. Ain't no excuse to be the way he is.* Zack thought to call out again but didn't, lest he cause people to come from the house to see what the shouting was about.

He had grained Biscuits and was nearly done brushing him when he heard footsteps. "Mr. Kotter, it was nice of you to stop by."

Zack turned around. It was full-on dark now. He had re-lit the lantern that the thin man had extinguished. At the edge of its light stood Mabel O'Keefe, a plump, rather plain looking woman with blonde hair who looked older than her 35 years by a good ten more. Her red and puffy eyes appeared cried out. She was wearing a bright yellow, ankle length dress. It had been Harley's favorite. Zack made eye contact with her, trying not to dwell on their condition he said, "I'm sorry to have missed Harley's service."

Mabel shook her head. "It's my fault. I shudda allowed folks more time but I needed to be done with it. A person can only cry for so long. I know Harley would understand."

"I reckon he would," said Zack, and then he purposely added to ease her conscience, "I know Harley wouldn't want ta burden you and yer youngsters with lottsa grievin'. You done the right thing."

A flicker of relief came to her eyes before she moved on. "Able said you got shot too."

Zack glanced down at his side. "It ain't as bad as it looks."

"Come up to the house. I'll give you a clean shirt and something to eat. I've got fried chicken and mashed potatoes. Got pumpkin pie too. Frank will likely have the milk separated here shortly so there'll be fresh cream for the pie."

"Frank?"

"Frank Harper, he said he ran into you down here."

"Oh, I didn't git his name."

"He can be that way at times."

Zack thought to say, *he strikes me as being that way all the time*, but he did not out of respect for Mabel and her circumstances. He said, "How was it that Harley came to hire Frank?"

Mabel shook her head slightly. "Well, you see how the land is getting carved up around here. Fencing what's yours is a sign of the times, don't you agree?"

"Yeah, I reckon I do but I was just curious as to where Harley ran into this Frank fella?"

"Him and his friend, Gerald, just showed up at the place one day wanting work. Harley needed help with fencing and putting up the hay so he hired the both of 'em."

"How they workin' out for ya?"

A puzzled look came to Mabel's face. "Why all the questions?"

Zack shrugged his shoulders. "I don't know. I guess the guy kinda rubbed me the wrong way."

"It's been a long day. Everyone is tired and maybe not at their best. And here it is dark and Frank is just finishing with the milking because -" Mabel's voiced cracked causing her to pause and recompose herself before going on, "because it took him some time to shovel the dirt over Harley."

It occurred to Zack that Able and Shorty could have helped, but he was hesitant to bring up their apparent absence so as to not put them in a bad light.

Mabel came back, as if she could read Zack's mind, "I told your friends to go home and tend to their chores. They protested leaving without helping to the point I threatened 'em with my broom. They'd done enough bringing Harley home and dressing him in his Sunday best and building a coffin. I couldn't ask anything more of them." She paused again, searching Zack's eyes for understanding. She added, "Come up to the house when you're done here. There's plenty to eat."

Zack felt embarrassed for casting aspersions on Frank. "That sounds mighty good, Mrs. O'Keefe. I'll be along shortly."

"Alright, I'll fix a plate for you and set it in the oven to warm."

"Much obliged Ma'am."

Supper was every bit as good as Zack had imagined it would be. Neighbors had brought enough food to feed Mabel and her family for a couple of days. There was, oddly, no talk of how Harley had died. It was as if they'd come together for some other innocuous reason and that all was bliss. But Zack could see it in their eyes, that white elephant in the room. He wondered when somebody amongst them would recognize it but no one did, not even Mabel's kids. They all pretended it wasn't there. At one point, her 12 year old daughter, Sarah, who was the spitting image of her mother, was trying especially hard to be stoic. She laughed, when no one else did, at an inane comment that Pastor Morgan had made. It was at that moment, when her laugh hung in the air seemingly louder than it was, that she became embarrassed. Tears had quickly started to fill her eyes, they were about to overflow when Zack, who had been among those who hadn't laughed, said in a jovial tone, *I don't mean ta be swinish Miss*

Sarah, but you reckon I could have a second piece ah that pie with a good amount ah cream on it. His comment contained her tears and kept the white elephant from taking center stage but it was Harley's youngest child, Teddy, that chased it right out of the room when he said, *You better be careful, Mr. Kotter, Pa says even a hog can bloat.* It was only then that everybody laughed as Mabel shushed her son.

The storm clouds that had formed over the O'Keefe place waited until just about midnight to release their burden. It was a gentle but steady rain that might not have awakened Zack had it not been for the thunder and lightning that came with it. For a good while, the thunder rolled over the mountains surrounding Harley's place like it was distant cannon fire. Lightning flashed again and again, illuminating the inside of the barn. Zack opened his eyes. He'd laid his bedroll in an empty stall. The sweet, pungent smell of horse manure was strong but it had not prevented him from going to sleep after all that he'd eaten at supper and a short glass of Harley's sipping whiskey. But now he was awake and right there with him was Harley, bleeding out on the road and Toby Sing's empty eye sockets and Li Ming and the riches she was willing to give him for her freedom. Just about everything that he'd been able to shed a few hours ago was now back, gnawing at him like a wolf pup on a bone. The wolf kept at it until shortly before sunup. And then, as luck would have it, or Zack's lack of, the rain quit, he fell back asleep and within minutes Frank was back to milk the cow again. Frank set the metal bucket down near the stall across from where Zack was sleeping. He allowed the handle to fold down and clank onto the rim of the bucket. Zack's eyes popped open.

"C'mon Flowers, you miserable old bitty," shouted Frank as he walked to the pasture behind the barn. "Let's git this over with."

Zack raised up on his elbows and looked around. He threw his blanket back. There was a damp chill in the air.

Even in the poor shadowy light within the barn he could see the cloud of his breath in front of him. His mind went to home and the likelihood that Shorty and General were, at that very moment, bringing in their milk cow. In the darkness of the stall he reached for his boots. He'd just finished putting them on when he heard the heavy, thudding steps of Flowers, a grayish Guernsey, coming into the barn. It was a familiar habit for her to go into the same stall, morning and night, and wait to have her milk drawn.

Frank poured a bucket of grain into the trough in front of Flowers so as to ensure her patience with the whole process. He was about to reach for his milking stool lying on the ground near the stall when he heard Zack rolling up his bedroll. He said, "Mornin'."

Zack responded in kind, "Mornin'." And then he finished tying the leather strings around his blankets and stood up, as he did he could see that Frank had not moved. It appeared he wanted to talk. Zack came back, "So yer a miner by trade?"

Frank scoffed. "Used ta be. It's a purty hit an' miss occupation. More missin' than hittin', generally."

"Well, I ain't never been much on bustin rocks. Reckon I'll stick with ranchin'"

Frank paused. It was clear to Zack that he was working up to something when he all of a sudden said, "So you got shot right along with Harley?"

"I got lucky."

"Yer friend Able told me you went to see the law about it."

Zack snorted. "Wouldn't you?"

Frank nodded. "I suppose, but the way yer friends tell it there ain't much for a lawman to go on. That kinda the way you see it?"

So now who's askin' too many questions? said Zack to himself. He said, leaving things as they were, "It is. It was a bushwhackin' pure and simple. Didn't see a thing. Sheriff said he might ride out this way sometime but, between me and you and the fence post, I wouldn't bet ya ah sarsaparilla on that happenin'."

Frank laughed politely and shook his head. "Helluva note that is, but I guess the man is just being practical in not wastin' his time comin' clear out here to look for what ain't there."

"Yeah, I reckon it is."

"I bet you'd like to catch up to these fellas, wouldn't ya?"

Zack scoffed. "Those boys may think they're in the clear, but they should know I'm like a hound on a lion track and I don't care how cold it is."

Frank's face went blank for a brief moment and then he said, "Sometimes that lion huntin' can be risky business." And then he reached for his milk bucket and stool. He took his place beside Flowers and began rhythmically pulling and squeezing her teats, the first streams of milk making a tinny sound as they collided with the bottom of the bucket. He had become, seemingly, oblivious to Zack's presence.

For a few seconds Zack stood where he was, looking at Frank's back and listening to the pulsating splashes of milk and Flowers grinding her oats. He thought to tell Frank that he was leaving to go up to the house for coffee, but he did not.

CHAPTER NINE

Zack stopped where he and Harley had been shot. The rain had not totally washed away Harley's blood. There were little, almost black crumbly clumps of soil where the blood had pooled. For a good while he sat there on Biscuits looking mostly up at the ridge where the shooters had been. He shook his head. *If I was of a mind ta kill somebody*, he said to himself, *I'd ah hid myself in these trees right next to the road. There'd be no doubt I'd hit my man.* And then it came to him, *this fella is real sure of his self. I'd bet he's cocky when it comes ta shootin'*.

Zack rode on, his mind was awash with competing thoughts, not the least of which was Li Ming's proposition. It was hard to fathom how he'd become concerned about a Chinese prostitute he didn't really even know and now, here she was offering him untold wealth if he would set her free. He was still wrestling with the potential consequences of all this as he came into sight of their place. General was first to spot him coming up the road. He came barking and running towards Zack until finally he fell in next to Biscuits where he excitedly kept pace.

Zack called down to him. "Oh, I missed you too, General dog. Yes I did." They went on in tandem like this, talking and barking until they arrived at the barn. Zack got down from Biscuits and knelt so General could lick his face. "Oh, what a good dog you are," he said as he ruffled General's ears.

"Thought maybe you decided to take up residence in the big city."

Zack looked up to see Able standing in the doorway of the barn with Shorty just beyond him sitting on the seat of the pedal powered grinding stone. Shorty hollered out as he held one of the cutters on the five-foot sickle bar to the revolving stone, "This damned rain has put a halt to the hay cuttin'."

Zack noted the yellow sparks coming off the grinder and that Shorty had raked the ground bare where they would be falling. He came back, in a loud voice so as to be heard over Shorty's commotion, "Well, I reckon the mower needed worked on anyway."

And then Able went right to it. "So, how'd it go with the law?"

Zack snorted and shook his head. "I believe we're purty much on our own. He said there's plenty a law-abiding folks that ride gray horses and shoot .44-100 rifles."

"What about that Chinese fella and that girl up at Elk Meadows? What'd he say about that?"

"Bickers and his boys say it was self defense and we don't. Their word against ours."

A smirk come to Able's face. "It don't matter that Bickers and his boys are lyin' scalawags of the worst kind and we're upstandin' citizens.?"

Zack laughed, as if to bleed off some of his frustration. "No, and Li Ming, she belongs to Bickers. She owes him a lotta money."

Shorty, who had stopped grinding so he could hear better, threw in, "I've heard ah such things."

Zack dug into his shirt pocket for Li Ming's map. He unfolded and handed it to Able. "How I come by this is a painful story I 'd just as soon not recount without the aid of some good whiskey, but the long and the short of it is, this is a map of where Toby Sing found gold. Li Ming got it to me and asked that I file a claim on this and get enough gold to buy her freedom from Bickers."

"And whatcha find after that?" asked Able.

Zack hesitated, not quite certain how he should answer Able, but then he said, "Well, it seems only right that we share it with her."

Able studied the map, turning it one way and then another. Finally, he said, looks like a school boy's doodles to me."

"Picture how Elk Meadows lays," said Zack. "Them little teepee marks is the mountains around the meadows. The squiggly lines is the criks."

"I see it," said Shorty who was now looking on. But then he laughed. "Having an X on a map and gold in yer pocket is two different things. I've known a number a fellas that's gone into a country that was a sure thing and they came away broke and hungry."

"It ain't like we'd be investin' our life savings in this," said Zack.

Able laughed. "That's fer damned sure cuz we already put that in this place."

Shorty came back. "I don't see how we can go lookin' for gold and do what needs ta be done around here, especially with all the thievin' that's going on."

Zack had expected Shorty and Able to be more receptive to Li Ming's proposal since there would be something in it for them. Their reluctance caused him to go quiet.

"If this was such a good deal why didn't Toby Sing just work this spot until he had enough to buy Li Ming?" asked Able in a somewhat challenging tone.

"You know a Chinaman can't file on an original claim," said Zack. "If he was to work this for any length of time, a white man would likely see him and just file on it and take it from him."

Shorty looked away and spit some tobacco juice. He came back, "I ain't got no desire to go into a mine shaft."

"I don't either," said Zack.

"And we ain't got the money to buy one of those big hydraulic nozzles ya see'em using to wash away whole mountains."

"How much does Li Ming owe Bickers?" asked Able.

Zack sighed, knowing the response he was likely to get. "Eleven hundred and fifty dollars."

Able laughed. "Hell, that's about what I made for the entire five years I was in the Army." He paused and shook his head before looking straight at Zack, "I heard in Placerville a while back that gold was going for 16 dollars an ounce. It'll take a lotta ounces to make $1,150, especially if we don't know how to go about gittin' it outta the ground."

"We could do it like the old-timers did with a pan and a sluice box," said Zack.

Shorty chimed in, "That's assuming the gold's in the crik. What if it's up in those steep-ass mountains around the meadows, then what?"

And then Able spit it out, "That Chinese whore has got you thinkin' too much with yer tallywhacker."

Zack shot Able an angry look but said nothing.

Able went on, "My thoughts on the matter is this is gonna take us away from what needs ta be done here and we might not even pay for our beans and coffee while we're up there lookin' for this gold. Winter 'll be here 'fore ya know it. We still got hay that needs ta be put up, elsewise we'll have starvin' livestock come January."

"If this was a sure thing," said Shorty, I'd be more apt to pitch in with ya but it ain't. I've spent time lookin' fer cows on that very crik this Chinaman put the X on. I've watered my horse there, studied deer tracks at the edge of it and I can tell ya I was not blinded by all the gold layin' around."

"You know how them Chinamen are," said Able, "they'll work for a nickel when ah white man wouldn't do the same thing for less than a dollar."

And then, as if their conversation had been a sudden gust of wind that died away as quick as it had come, they went silent, seemingly confident that they'd made their case.

Zack allowed the silence to envelope them. In that moment he wondered if Able wasn't right about Li Ming, that her beauty had clouded his thinking. He actually didn't even know her yet, and here he was allowing this concern or infatuation he had for her to jeopardize his relationship with men he'd known for a little over eight years. And then the naysayer in his mind shouted at him, *you fool, she's just a whore. You wouldn't have anything with her anyway.* Nonetheless, to his surprise, he said, "Give me a week, boys. If it don't look promising after that, I'll drop the whole matter."

Shorty and Able exchanged looks. Neither wanted to be hardnosed about it but there was work to be done before winter. Able said, in a firm tone, "One week, Zack. That's it."

Zack nodded, "I'm obliged fellas. Consider this a grubstake. I'll cut ya in if anything comes of it."

Shorty laughed. "I'll settle for a promise of a steak supper and a stiff drink in town sometime."

Zack forced himself to smile, as it struck him how little confidence they had in what he was proposing to do.

CHAPTER TEN

It was not the sendoff he would have liked. In fact, it wasn't a sendoff at all as Able and Shorty were mostly indifferent to Zack's leaving for Elk Meadows. At breakfast they talked mostly about finishing up the haying and checking on their horses that were running on the open ridges above the South Fork of the Payette, and the calves that still needed to be branded, and wondering if the rustlers were going to leave them alone now, and just about anything but Zack going to look for gold so he could buy a Chinese whore her freedom. If their intent had been to flood his conscience with guilt for leaving them with all the work, they had succeeded. He had thought, to redeem himself just a little, that he would do the breakfast dishes but, when he still had half a hotcake and a slice of bacon yet to eat, Shorty shoveled in the last of his food and picked up his plate and silverware and got up from the table. He headed straight for the big tin wash pan hanging on the wall to the left of the stove.

Zack called out. "Shorty, sit yerself down. I'll do the dishes."

Shorty came back in a voice that was absent of any suggestion he wanted to banter in a good-natured way, he said simply, "That's alright. I'll tend to it."

Zack stared at Shorty, thinking he would turn around but he did not. *That old cuss purposely didn't eat as much as he usually does just so he could be first done and shame me for not doing the dishes.*

And then Able, pretending to be oblivious to what was going on, finished the last of his food and got up from the table. He said to Shorty, "I'll roundup the team for the mower 'fore I go."

Shorty, who had set the pan on the counter beneath some shelves on the west end of the room, was now pouring hot water in it from a large metal coffee pot that he'd taken from the stove. He hollered over his shoulder, "I'll have supper ready when you git back tonight."

Able said, his tone bitter, "Hopefully, our horses are still there."

Shorty snorted, but did not look up from the skillet he had begun to wash. "Wouldn't that be nice."

"Yes sir, it would." And with that Able left without so much as glancing at Zack.

It had been hurtful to not be a part of the conversation this morning and now with it being just him and Shorty in the silence of the cabin, save for the occasional popping of the stove, it had gotten downright uncomfortable for Zack. He was about to challenge Shorty on how he and Able had been when Shorty said, still not looking at him, "I hope ya find ah ton ah gold up there, Zack. Able does too, but just know that it's an all or nothing deal."

"How so?"

Shorty turned around to face Zack. "This ranch was what we talked about nearly everyday when we was in the Army. And now we've got it, or at least we're building it up, and you wanna go chasin' after gold to buy some Chinese whore her freedom. I reckon it's all fine and dandy you wantin' ta git this girl away from that Bickers fella, but we got a ranch to take care of and you can't do that and be a miner at the same time."

"I don't care ta be a miner, Shorty. If I go up to Elk Meadows and find eleven hundert and fifty dollars worth ah gold tomorrow, I'd quit and not tell a soul where I got it from. Wadin' around in ah crik and scoopin' gravel up is not how I want ta spend my life."

Shorty laughed and shook his head. "Well then, I guess this Chinese girl must be a real looker to have you snagged the way she does."

"I can't explain it fer certain, Shorty. Li Ming is darned sure ah purty girl but it goes beyond that. I guess I feel sorry for the fix she's in."

Shorty laughed again, the tenor of it being sarcastic, he said, "You may have yer own fix ta git out of if you keep going the way you are."

Zack stood up and went to the door, as he opened it he paused and looked at Shorty, "One week and I hope to have this business behind me."

Shorty looked at Zack but offered no words of encouragement, nothing, before he went back to washing dishes.

Zack had spent the day before rounding up everything that he and General would need to be gone for a week. He'd brought the panniers to the house to load as there, and the root cellar next to it, were where most everything was located. He had led Jones, an old mule the Army had deemed as no longer fit for service, to the house to pick up the panniers. He was in the process of hefting the panniers onto Jones' packsaddle when he saw Able come out the barn and get onto his horse. Given the way things had gone this morning, Zack did not wave or continue looking in Able 's direction. Nonetheless, he hoped, half expected that Able would ride over to the house and say goodbye. He did not.

The rain clouds that hung over the area day before yesterday had moved on. It was sunny and warm and would have made for a pleasant ride to Elk Meadows, had it not been for all the turmoil in Zack's mind. It bothered him considerably that he had alienated Able and Shorty. Their response had taken him by surprise. It was like they viewed him as a fool, naïve enough to believe there was a fortune in gold awaiting them in a place countless other prospectors had likely gone over before Toby Sing. And then his thoughts came full circle, *they're right, I've allowed myself to become smitten by a purty girl I hardly know.*

He did not want to go past Toby Sing's campsite or where he was buried, but it was on the most direct route to where the X on the map was. He paused and looked over at the grave, it was intact, just as he and Able had left it. And then the events of that day came back to him. It sent a shiver over his body that caused him to jerk around in his saddle, half expecting to see an apparition of those players. But they were not there, just a gust of wind and the shrill caws of a raven flying overhead. He urged Biscuits on. It wasn't like he was ever totally free of those images but, at times, they were diluted with other thoughts. Within a few minutes he came to a little no-name trickle of water, barely three feet wide running down the bottom of a shallow draw that started up in the rocks beyond the dark timber surrounding the meadow. Willows and a few Quaking Aspen gave away its presence, that otherwise from a distance would have been a secret. Zack sat on Biscuits looking down at the tiny creek. He studied it as if now it would look different to him than the other times that he'd been here rounding up cattle. The water had not the slightest impurity. It was as clear as absolute nothingness, but still, he could not see the gold. Gravel, that sometimes became cobble rock, lay beneath the water. It was colorful, white, orange-ish and creamy smooth like jasper, and purples and reds. But there was no yellow, nothing that looked like gold.

Zack sighed, he said looking down at General who was patiently sitting beside the water watching the darting movements of a fingerling trout. "Well General, it's gonna be dark in a coupla hours so I reckon we better git our camp set up."

General looked around in response to Zack's voice and the fact Biscuits had started up the creek towards the timber. He quickly caught up and passed them.

It was tempting to unsaddle Biscuits and Jones and take the gold pan and look for the yellow amongst the other colored rocks, but he did not. When he'd asked Shorty if he could borrow the pan that had hung out in the blacksmith part of the barn since they'd built it several years ago, Shorty had responded sarcastically, *sure, you can have the damned thing. I got no need for it.* Zack figured Shorty's gruffness was due to embarrassment from his changed attitude and the current situation. It may have been too, that he had looked for gold and failed to find any, regardless, Zack did not draw attention to the fact that Shorty's outlook on life was less practical when he had acquired the pan than it was now.

The sun was no longer visible by the time he got Biscuits and Jones brushed and grained and picketed where there was good grass and built his lean-to from the canvas tarp that he had brought for that purpose. It was definitely too dark to look for yellow rocks, or what he hoped would be gold. It occurred to him that he could build a fire close to the creek, as he'd seen the Chinese do in the old tailings down near Idaho City, and work by its light. But then he laughed at himself. *Hell, I ain't for sure what I'm lookin' for in broad daylight let alone a campfire.* He considered just brewing some coffee and share some of the pemmican that he had brought for General and go to bed. It was good pemmican, he'd made it himself from venison, thimbleberries and beef fat. Finally, however, he rekindled his ambition and peeled some spuds and fried some bacon and ate that with some biscuits and chokecherry jam from home. All that and some black coffee left him pleasantly satiated as he and General sat on the blankets beneath the lean-to looking out at the flickering flames of the fire and beyond it to where, not long ago, Toby and Li Ming had likely shared a moment beside their campfire, and more. The thought of it bothered him some but then, in the next instant, he saw the terror in her face as the both of them lay on the floor of the Ore Chute. In time, the fire died away to glowing red embers allowing the darkness to move in closer. Zack crawled out from the lean-to and stood up, going into the night where he stopped to relieve himself, as he did, he looked up at the stars. They were like illuminated grains of sand. In a way, they evoked a feeling of never-ending loneliness in Zack. It, once again, caused him to shiver and look around, out into the darkness. It was quiet, so quiet that it begged for anything, an owl or coyote even, to break the silence, but none did. When he had finished, he went back to his shelter and crawled between his blankets with General lying beside him and his pistol near at hand. He sighed, *six more days.*

Not quite all of the stars had retreated from the sky when Zack finally surrendered to his inability to sleep. A light frost coated the grass and his breath hung in the air before him, reminders that fall was here and he should be helping with the haying instead of doing what he was. On the ride here yesterday he'd gone over in his mind what an old prospector had showed him about panning for gold. It had been a chance meeting, several years ago, on a little creek that ran into the Payette. He'd been hunting deer when he stumbled upon the man, squatting at the edge of the water, staring down into his pan as he rocked and swirled it in a steady motion. For a time, his attention to the gravel in his pan caused him to be unaware of Zack's presence but then, from the corner of his eye, he caught sight of Zack and quickly set the pan down as if what he was doing was a secret. They exchanged pleasantries as each rolled a smoke and told one another what news they'd heard of late until, out of curiosity,

Zack asked, *how is it you can separate the gold from the rest of those rocks?*

At first, the old man seemed hesitant to say but finally he came back, *gold settles out on account of being heavier than the rest of it.* He then took another drag from his cigarette and blew the smoke out over the gurgling water like he had no more to say about the subject.

In retrospect, Zack was now glad that he had persisted, *can ya show me how ya work the pan?*

The old man had frowned. *My intention is ta file a claim on this part ah the crik so I hope you ain't got any designs on it.*

Zack laughed. *I'm ah cow man.*

The old prospector removed the cigarette from his mouth all the while staring at Zack as if to assess his true motive. Still mute, he flicked his tongue out and snatched a bit of tobacco on his lower lip and then expelled it into the space before him. Finally, apparently satisfied that Zack's interest was genuine curiosity, he said, *I'll show ya one time how it's done.* He then got up from the log where he had been sitting and scooped a shovel full of gravel from the shallow stream and dumped it in his pan. *Ya got ta have a good amount of water,* he said as he dipped the pan in the slow-moving current. *After ya got yer water and gravel ya just start workin' yer pan side ta side and rockin' it so yer gravel mixes up real good with the water. By and by, you bleed off the rocks and sand and water until all you got left is the gold, if there is any.*

On that day, Zack recalled when the old man was done working his pan, there was a speck of gold about the size of a pin head in the bottom of it. He'd spent close to 20 minutes washing it out of the gravel which didn't seem to bother him. Zack smiled but stopped short of laughing. *Ain't gonna be too much competition for this claim, I reckon.* The old man glanced up at Zack, as if to gauge his trustworthiness one more time before pulling a small pill bottle from his shirt pocket. He removed its cork stopper and then carefully pinched the bit of gold between his thumb and index finger and dropped it in the bottle. Zack remembered him pushing the cork back in so tight he'd said to himself, *he's gonna play hell gittin' that out.* And now, here he was three years later with his own little bottle and a borrowed gold pan.

Zack's desire to test his skill at panning was such that breakfast became a formality of coffee and a cold biscuit with some preserves. It reminded him of those forced marches with Custer when that's all they got, minus the preserves.

"C'mon General, time ta go ta work."

General was lying on the ground just beyond the ring of rocks enclosing the fire. He was chewing contentedly on a stick, but let it go seeing that Zack had gotten to his feet.

Zack picked up the shovel which was leaning across the pack saddle to the left of his lean-to, and mixed the fire with the soil beneath it until it was a smoldering patch of ashes. "Alright, General dog, let's see what riches this little crik is willin' ta give up."

General led the way as if he knew the best place to begin, with Zack trailing along carrying his pan and shovel. In spite of the bad blood back at the ranch, Zack was excited to try his hand at gold panning. They'd just come out of the trees and into the meadow when Zack angled over towards a spot on the creek that was lacking brush or trees. Instead, its banks were thick with grasses and brown-topped sedges that made for a heavy sod. He stopped at the very edge of the water and peered down into it. It was no different than what he'd seen yesterday, just more multi-colored rocks, none of which appeared to be gold. He dropped the pan, right side up, into the lush grass. General, curious as to what was going on, sat down near the pan as Zack leaned out with his shovel and scooped up some gravel, only to have about half of it washed away before he could bring it to the surface. The water was no more than eight or nine inches deep, but at this particular location it was moving at a good clip. Zach sighed. "It's a start, General." Setting the shovel aside, he dropped to his knees in the grass, which was wet from last night's frost. Its coldness instantly penetrated his cotton pants complimenting the fact that he could still see his breath in the air. To the east, the sun was but a sliver on the horizon giving no promise of warmth anytime soon.

Zack prodded his memory to that day with the old miner. *Got ta git a good amount of water in the pan*, he said to himself as he dipped the edge of it in the creek. And then he began, rocking the pan from side to side, roiling the finer gravel and sand into a cloudy mix while the bigger rocks just tumbled around. After a minute or so, he set the pan down and plucked the rocks too big to be gently washed out by tilting the pan. He then went back to rocking and swirling the water and the fine sand and gravel suspended in it until, finally, he felt confident that he would not be losing gold. Already, the cold air, cold water and cold steel of the pan had numbed his hands making it more difficult to carefully finesse the worthless gravel and sand over the lip of the pan. It was a slow tedious process that had taken every bit as long as the old man, if not longer, but he was down to about a coffee cup of muddy water mixed in with some fine matter when he saw it, just a flash of yellow. But then, as quick as he'd seen it, the cloudy water covered it over. Zack's heart began to pound. Between his excitement and the cold, it became difficult to control the pan. Swirling, rocking and then shaking the pan from side to side until finally there it was, a piece of gold bigger than the old man's but not by much. Zack was consumed with elation that even now was already hinting at, *I told you so.* He set the pan down so the muddy water would drain away to the far side of it, leaving the fine sandy gravel and the speck of gold. And then just as the old man had done, he fished an empty medicine bottle from his shirt pocket. Gingerly, he attempted to pick up the chunk of gold with his numb, trembling fingers. It took three tries before he could pluck it from the grit and drop it safely in his bottle. He held the bottle up towards the glow of the partially exposed sun on the far side of the basin and looked at the tiny granule of gold. He laughed at himself. "We're miners, General. Our very first pan and we got gold. Why, we do this till dark we might have something to show for ourselves." And then he laughed again, his demeanor having become almost giddy. For a moment, this feeling prevailed until the naysayer within him spoke up, *this speck of gold is a longways from eleven hundert an' fifty dollars*. Doubt began to roll over Zack's enthusiasm like the incoming tide, getting higher and higher until suddenly it was covered. *Ya damned fool, yer riskin' everything for this woman and to what end*? Undeterred, the naysayer railed on, attacking a fantasy that he had begun to allow himself, *ain't never gonna be anything between you and her, for three dollars she's anybody's girl*. Then there was laughter and taunts, some of it faceless and some of it not, until finally, Zack stood and took up the shovel. He drove it deep into the colorful water-smoothed rocks and pried back on it. "We got ta see it through, General."

At the end of the day, he had worked 31 pans. Slightly less than half of them contained any gold. His excitement had succumbed to reality. And so it began, a litany of repetition, hopefulness with the dawning of a new day that this would be the day when a big nugget would turn up in his pan or the gold specks would outnumber the worthless rocks. Each night he dreamed of these riches and sometimes of the physical pleasures that Li Ming could afford him. But he could not sustain these dreams as his seemingly newfound common sense would awaken and then berate him for having been so foolish. It made for long nights. His boots and clothes were perpetually wet and muddy. He tried to dry them near the fire but the cold, damp mountain air made it difficult. Steam would rise up from his things and they would be hot and damp to the touch. By morning, when the fire was nothing but warm ashes, his clothes were cold and stiff. Putting his boots on, which had shrunk after the first day from wading in the water, now represented one of his biggest physical challenges each day. The weather had definitely turned more fall-like. In the mornings, there was a skiff of ice at the edges of the tiny stream where the water was slow and shallow. In the shady parts of the creek the ice persisted till early afternoon, but was generally gone by mid-morning in the sunny places. Zack had told himself, *this misery would be more tolerable if I had somethin' ta show for it.*

It was the sixth day, his last day for panning. Zack removed the stopper from his little medicine bottle as he sat on the blankets under his lean-to and carefully poured the bits of gold into a teaspoon. He snorted, "Hell, General, I betcha we ain't even got an ounce. Maybe two-thirds of an ounce if we're lucky."

General, who was laying on the blankets next to Zack with his head resting on his front paws did not look up. He was no doubt content to just lay there since he'd just finished his breakfast.

Zack sighed and poured the gold back into his bottle. *At this rate, I'll be two or three years earnin' $1,150.00.* He shook his head and said aloud, "What am I doin' here?" He picked up his cup, which was sitting on the ground in front of him, and took a couple of swallows of the coffee that had become cold before tossing the rest onto the fire. "Time ta go ta work, General."

The creek with the X on it was about three quarters of a mile long from where it started up high in the rocks surrounding the basin, to where it emptied into the bigger creek in the middle of the meadows. Until today, Zack had worked that part of the creek out in the meadow since it was not in the shade of the tall timber. But this morning, after having just looked at the results of working the past four days in the meadow he decided to go into the timber. *Maybe that's where Toby Sing found the good stuff*, he said to himself.

The little creek had nurtured the big pine trees to an even larger stature than those in the drier parts of the basin. On a hot summer day their shade would be most welcome, but it was almost ten o'clock in the morning in late September and Zack could still see his breath in the air. He had just worked his tenth pan with results no more favorable than the meadow and its sunshine had offered up. The realization that what Toby Sing had viewed as a rich claim would yield, at best, only a meager living, was a hard truth for Zack to accept. So far, it looked like it wouldn't pay much more than fifty or sixty dollars a month and that was while the gold lasted. Cold and dejected, he sat down on an old log that lay parallel to the creek. It had sloughed off most of its bark and turned a silver-gray years ago giving it a hard, slick appearance until it got out close to 50 feet where it became rotten and crumbly. The decaying inner wood had turned a rusty brown in contrast to the rest of the log. Zack took out his Bull Durham and papers and began rolling himself a cigarette which was no easy task given the fact his fingers were so numb they had little sensation in them. Finally, his fumbling succeeded and he drew in the acrid smoke, savoring it until, at last, he spewed it out before him. He sat quietly, resting his elbows on his knees, staring at the gurgling little creek that had betrayed him. Mountain chickadees were singing nearby. In the distance, an occasional raven or Steller's jay called out.

"General, tomorrow we'll be shed ah this place."

General, who was laying near Zack's feet, suddenly looked intently across the creek and into the wall of green trees. No sooner had he done this than a pine squirrel, not far into the sea of green, let out its high-pitched staccato chatter. It caused General to growl, which he usually never did in response to squirrels. Zack's heartbeat ratcheted up a notch. *Could be a lion or bear*, he said to himself. But then he stood and looked around as the more likely possibility of what disturbed the squirrel commandeered his mind's eye. *Indians ain't caused no trouble in these parts in some time. Probably some damned fool that thinks I'm gittin' rich sievin' the gold outta these rocks and so he figures ta take it from me.* The trees and brush in all directions afforded anyone, man or beast, good cover. Zack had just retreated beyond the gray log when a familiar voice sounded behind him.

"Well, if it isn't the cowboy." An evil laugh followed.

Zack spun around. Anger instantly flooded his body. He called out, in a sarcastic tone, "You come ta pay yer respects ta Toby?"

Hyrum Bickers snorted and tossed his head back slightly. "You ruined my girl. She's got some fool notion that she can buy her freedom."

Zack smiled derisively. "Maybe she can."

"Not by your hand, she won't."

"You never know. This little crik is provin' ta be purty rich."

Bickers' eyes lit up in a sinister way. "It don't matter how much gold is here, Li Ming is gone."

"Whaddaya sayin?"

"I'm sayin' she's gone to parts unknown. More 'n likely someplace you'll never find her." And then Bickers laughed on purpose so as to goad Zack into doing something irrational.

"Who'd ya sell her to?"

Bickers laughed again, knowing that it would make Zack even more angry. "You write out a statement saying you relinquish your right to file on this claim and I'll tell ya."

"That still leaves Li Ming owin' some scoundrel, most likely, for her freedom. Why don't you do the decent thing and just tell me."

"Hell's gonna freeze over 'fore I tell you that."

Zack knew the answer but he asked anyway, "Then why is it yer here?"

"Whores ain't good at keepin' secrets. It didn't sit too well with me when I heard you'd come up here to stake that Chinaman's gold strike so's you could buy Li Ming. This was right after I'd sold her paper for a lot less than I gave for her just so I could be rid of the whiny bitch. So, I'm here to recoup my losses."

Zack looked at Bickers in an angry, hateful way, "Well, that ain't gonna happen."

"It appears to me," said Bickers with a taunting smirk on his face, "that whoever gits back to town first and files on this will be the fella countin' his gold."

"Ya gotta pound some stakes in the ground ta mark the corners 'fore you can file and I'm here ta tell ya, you'll play hell gittin' that done as long as I'm here."

Bickers snorted, still maintaining an evil smile. "There's a simple remedy for that. You ain't gonna like it but it suits me just fine."

Fear gripped Zack. His heart was pounding painfully hard. He knew what was coming. Even if he'd viewed himself as some kind of a gunfighter, he would have been afraid as his hands were numb from panning in the cold water. The Army had not trained him to be a quick draw but rather stay calm and make your shots count. He called out to Bickers who was standing at the edge of the trees on the other side of the creek, "I figured this would be yer style, but at least I'm gittin' more chance than Toby Sing."

Bickers scoffed. "I see ya buried the Chinaman, but don't you go thinkin' I'll do the same for you. I'm gonna leave ya for the vermin."

From where Zack stood, it would be about a 70 or 80 foot shot. His mind was racing. *I gotta be movin' or he'll hit me dead center sure as hell.*

Suddenly, the sarcastic, taunting look left Bickers' face. He brushed his coat back behind the holster on his right hip. He looked Zack straight in the eye, "Alright cowboy, whenever yer ready to die, make yer move."

Bickers had barely finished with his hateful bravado when Zack dove to the ground behind the gray log. In that instant he heard the report of Bickers' pistol and seconds later it roared again splintering the wood just above Zack's head. Somehow, on his way to the ground, he had managed to get his own pistol out but now he was pinned down. Abruptly, it became quiet, save for some ravens off in the distance. It was like the lonely tranquility of the meadows was unchanged. And then he heard it, the crackling of ice breaking and the sloshing of water. Zack took a deep breath to calm himself. *He's comin'. I gotta move and then just pop up and take my shot* or he'll *walk in on me and shoot me like a wounded animal.* Zack turned to his stomach to crawl to a new position along the log when General erupted with a deluge of savage growl-like barks and started towards Bickers.

Bickers turned his pistol in General's direction, "Why you damned mutt." But then from the corner of his eye he saw that Zack had sat up from behind the log. Terror came to his eyes as he shifted his aim towards Zack who was now partially shrouded in the black smoke that had poured from the barrel of his pistol. It was a dead man's reflex that enabled Bickers to get off one more shot that would have hit Zack in the belly had it not been for the log. The bullet from Zack's .45 struck Bickers in the heart. Its impact caused him to pitch backwards, leaving his upper torso in the creek.

Zack stood up, as he did General came running to him coming to a stop with his front paws up on the old gray log. Zack leaned over and allowed General to lick his face while he ruffled his ears. "Yer a good dog, General. Yes, you are. You saved my bacon. There'll be extra pemmican for you tonight." In Zack's mind, there was little doubt that General had recognized the gravity of the situation.

A wave of intense shivering, trembling almost, swept over Zack as he looked at Bickers lying there, half in and half out of the creek. He blamed the cold for some of it but mostly it was the adrenaline rush, the giddy relief that General had distracted Bickers and knowing that if he hadn't, he'd be the one lying dead on the ground.

Although he had little doubt that Bickers would not have done the same for him, Zack dug a grave and buried Bickers near the creek. It wasn't as deep as Toby Sing's, but it was better than nothing.

CHAPTER ELEVEN

After he had killed Bickers, just being in Elk Meadows gave Zack an uncomfortable feeling. In the past before he'd witnessed Toby Sing's murder, and now this, it had been a nice place to go, but not anymore. His uneasiness with the aura that hung over the basin, and the fact that he would have to go back to Idaho City and tell the sheriff his side of things, caused him to break camp and head out with only a few hours of light left in the day. *I can at least git through the notch 'fore dark*, he'd told himself.

It was dusk the next day when he arrived back at the ranch. Travel had been slower than usual due to his having Bickers' horse and mule in tow. His conscience wouldn't allow him to leave them picketed in the big timber with no one ever coming back for them. Light was visible from inside their cabin while blue smoke lazed in the air above it, suggesting to Zack that Shorty and Able had likely cooked supper. *I wonder if they made any extra*, he said to himself. *Today is the seventh day I been gone. They knew I was comin back today.* As he stepped down from Biscuits, he heard loud voices and then laughter coming from the cabin. It struck him as odd, but he had animals to tend to.

He'd relieved the horses and mules of their burdens and was just starting to brush them when he saw the cabin door open spilling a shaft of light into the front yard. Straightaway, the yellow light filled with the outlines of three men walking towards the barn and corrals. Two of the shapes Zack recognized right off as Shorty and Able, but the third, who was trailing behind them, went into the darkness before he figured out who he was. Zack continued brushing Biscuits, occasionally glancing over his back at the approaching men. It came to him, *I guess things ain't changed any since I left. I been here a good ten minutes and this is the first they come outta the house.* He could hear a murmuring of competing voices followed by an outburst of laughter.

And then as the trio drew near, Zack could see who the third person was. A surge of fear shot through his body. He called out, "Evenin' Sheriff."

Sheriff Snyder stopped abruptly, looking not at Zack but Bickers' horse and mule. He studied the animals for a moment, as if to make certain of their identity, before shifting his eyes to Zack. "It appears Hyrum Bickers found you."

Zack rested both of his hands on Biscuits' back and looked over at Snyder. "He did and then he tried to kill me so's he could be first ta file on this piddling claim I was workin'."

"I didn't figure you to come out on top of this affair."

"Neither did I, but I reckon you know it was him that came after me."

"I do. One of the whores at the Ore Chute got word to me last night of what Bickers was up to. Said she gave up Li Ming's secret, but only after Bickers beat her."

"So, is it true, Bickers sold Li Ming?"

Snyder laughed. "Is that what he told you?"

Zack nodded. "Yeah, he made a point ah tellin' me she was goin' someplace where I'd never find her."

The Sheriff shrugged and shook his head slightly. "I can't say where she went to, but I'm certain it wasn't of her own accord. Oh, and Bickers lost her in a poker game."

Zack snorted. "I didn't figure he'd sell her."

Pointing towards Bickers' horse and mule, Snyder said, "Those animals belong to the livery in town. The tack too."

"What about his personal stuff, guns and such?"

"I reckon you can keep it."

"I don't want it."

"Alright, I'll take it all back with me in the morning."

A look of apprehension came to Zack's face but his voice hinted at defiance, "What about me? Where do you and I stand?"

Snyder looked almost indifferent. "I guess I could go out to Elk Meadows and dig up Bickers and perform an inquest like he was some upstanding citizen and there was this big mystery about how he died, but I ain't gonna do that. From what I know of you, I don't believe you're the kinda fella ta shoot a man in the back. What I do believe is that Bickers rode out there with the intention of killing you and it backfired on him."

"So, we're square?"

"As far as I'm concerned, we are. But, when it comes to one of Bickers' cronies or a relative wanting to even the score, I can't say that one of 'em won't come after ya."

The possibility that Bickers would have somebody that cared enough about him and was of the moral caliber to kill another man out of vengeance had not occurred to Zack. With all that had already happened, it only added to the angst brewing within him, he said, "Guess I better watch my back trail for a while."

Shorty shook his head. "Ain't never gonna be any damned peace around here. I guess it's just too much ta ask for a fella ta just work hard and make a livin'."

The fact that neither Able or Shorty had said a word up to this point in the conversation had not been lost on Zack. There didn't appear to be any concern for what might happen to him or what he'd been forced to do at Elk Meadows. He said, not really caring if his apology rang true, "I'm sorry ta bring trouble to you boys. Hopefully, it won't come to that."

Able scoffed. "It already has, Zack. Me an' Shorty been tendin' ta business while you been off lookin' fer gold to buy a whore that's left the country, and now here ya are maybe crosswise with a dead man's kin. We don't need it."

"It ain't yer fight, if it even comes to that."

Able laughed briefly in a derisive tone. "I'll remember that if there comes a gun fight when I'm with you." And with that Able turned away and started towards the house with Shorty close behind.

Zack and the Sheriff watched them leave until they were mostly absorbed into the darkness and then the Sheriff said, "They're concerned about ya. It's all they talked about at supper. They just don't understand this thing you've got for Li Ming."

Zack sighed. "I'm not sure I do either."

CHAPTER TWELVE

On the ride back yesterday, Zack had made considerable progress towards convincing himself that Bickers had been lying to him about Li Ming being gone. The idea of it had come fairly easy to him due to Bickers being who he was, but now the sheriff had changed all that. In his mind, the urgency to help Li Ming had finally surrendered to common sense. *Hell, I don't even know where she's gone to*, he said to himself. It was as if Li Ming had become a phantom and everybody, Shorty, Able, Snyder and Zack, they all recognized it as close to fact. But then, when they were mostly done eating breakfast, Shorty brought her back to life, he said looking across the table to the Sheriff, "Musta been ah helluva poker game for Bickers to have lost that high-priced Chinese gal."

Able laughed. "I didn't think there was anybody in Idaho City with that kinda money. Why I betcha on any given night you could pool the money of every customer in that saloon ah Bickers and not come up with-" Able paused and looked at Zack, "How much did you say she owed Bickers?"

"Eleven hundert an' fifty dollars."

"I didn't witness the game myself," said Snyder, "but, what I heard was it had been friendly for most of the night until they'd drank a little too much whiskey and then the betting got plum outta hand."

Shorty laughed so as to insert himself into the Sheriff's narrative, "Musta been some mighty good whiskey."

Snyder smiled politely and then went on, "The game shrunk down to just Bickers and some stranger. Now, what was told to me was they both had world beater hands and that one of'em would bet and the other one would raise 'im until finally this stranger pulls out five hundred dollars cash money and raises Bickers."

Zack's suspicion caused him to blurt out, "Why, what kinda fool carries around that much money on his person?"

Snyder's tone became sheriff-like, "More to the point, how does a fella come by that kind of money? I'm thinkin' Bickers ran into one of his own kind." Snyder paused briefly to allow the meaning of his words to sink in, and then he went on, "Now, as it was told to me, Bickers couldn't cover the bet –"

"He didn't have that kind ah money on hand at the bar?" asked Zack incredulously.

Snyder came back, his expression was like he had something profound to say, "Boys, I'm here ta tell ya, Idaho City ain't no garden of prosperity, not even when it comes ta sellin' liquor and women, it ain't."

Having done the math, Zack scoffed, "So, he gave up Li Ming's contract worth over a thousand dollars to call a five hundred dollar bet?"

Snyder grinned. "A full house, kings over queens will make a fella do such things."

"Well, what'd the other fella have?" prodded Able.

Snyder laughed like he had no sympathy whatsoever for Bickers. "Four deuces, can ya believe it. I'll betcha ole Bickers thought he was on thick ice with that full boat. I'd like ta seen the look on his face when that other guy turned over all them deuces."

They all laughed along with Snyder, none of them caring about Bickers' loss while holding a seemingly unbeatable hand. And none of them, except Zack, appeared concerned about Li Ming's fate. For the others, it apparently hadn't crossed their mind, until Zack said, "How did Li Ming take to all this?"

The momentum of the conversation caused Snyder to say with a casual indifference, "Damned if I know." Almost immediately, he saw the anger come to Zack's eyes and corrected himself, in a contrite tone, "The fella recitin' these events didn't say." But then he offered up, "Bein' outta that sportin' house ought ta please her, don't ya reckon?"

Shorty snorted. "Hell, it's second nature to some of those gals."

Zack glared at Shorty. "That's a damned fool thing ta say and you know it."

Shorty looked at Zack and frowned. He appeared to have something to say in response but then, abruptly, he got up from the table, sighed heavily and shook his head in disgust as he walked over to the stove for more coffee.

A quiet tension suddenly engulfed them. Sitting on the counter across the room was a brass alarm clock, its loud ticking drawing attention to how things were. On it went, tick, tick, tick until finally, Snyder rescued them, standing he said, "Boys, I'm much obliged for the hospitality but its time for me to be makin' tracks."

Able remained seated as he looked up at the Sheriff. "Appreciate yer stopping by even if it wasn't ta tell us ya got ah handle on the rustlers in these parts."

A hint of insult came to Snyder's eyes but he let it go no further. "These scoundrels will slip up one day and when they do, I'll acquaint them with the hospitality of the territorial prison."

Shorty, who was still standing near the stove sipping on his coffee, did not hold back with his bitterness as to how things were. "We can't abide any more losses, Sheriff. Just so ya know, if I run on to one ah these sons-ah-bitches I am to put a permanent end to his career."

Snyder looked hard at Shorty. "This ain't the old days, Shorty. The law's got boundaries. You need ta respect'em."

And then Zack, seeing that Shorty's mouth was a train about to derail itself, jumped in, "Sheriff, I'll help ya catch up yer stock."

Snyder had not yet shifted his eyes from Shorty to Zack when Zack pressed on, the pace of his words being quick, "I saw that big black mule ah yers in the pasture last night. That's ah fine lookin' animal. Is she ornery?"

The Sheriff hesitated for another second or two, his eyes fixed on Shorty so as to make his point, before acknowledging Zack. "No sir, she packs real good. Generally, she don't give me a minute's worth a trouble." He then turned towards the door purposely not offering to shake any hands.

After going outside the two of them continued on with the idle talk about mule behavior, so as to fill the stillness of the morning, until they were out of earshot of the cabin and then Snyder came back with what needed to be said, "I won't tolerate a lotta vigilantism. You need ta convince yer pardner of that fact. It can get outta hand. I've seen more 'n once where the wrong folks has got hanged."

"Well Sheriff," said Zack with a definite edge in his voice, "you saw what happened ta me an' Harley."

"That's different. You got a right to defend yerself, but you cross the line when you decide if a fella is guilty of something and what his punishment should be. It's up to a judge and jury to make that call."

"You, and any judge and jury is a good ways from here." Zack paused, knowing that Snyder would take offense if he said what he was thinking but, in the next instant, the words escaped him. "Maybe if we was ta see a little more a you out here we'd have a more favorable take on how you see things as needin' ta happen."

"Well, I'm here now, ain't I?"

It had not been Zack's intention to get in a debate with Snyder, especially since his reason for being there had been to stop Bickers from killing him and stealing Toby Sing's claim. Nonetheless, he felt compelled to make it clear to the Sheriff how things were for the ranchers in the area. He came back with a left-handed apology of sorts, "I didn't mean ta slam the door on yer tail so I hope ya don't take offense, it's just we're purty frustrated with losin' our stock to these rustlers."

Snyder's demeanor appeared to soften, he said, "I came prepared to spend a few days out here, nose around a bit, see what I can turn up on this fella that rides a gray horse."

Zack nodded. "I appreciate that Sheriff. Maybe yer being here will scare these thieves enough that they'll quit the country."

The Sheriff smiled and scoffed, "Ain't nobody that scared a me."

CHAPTER THIRTEEN

After getting directions to Harley O'Keefe's place, Sheriff Snyder set out, but not before promising Zack that he would tell no one about the claim Zack had staked in Elk Meadows. At least not until Zack had filed on it, which would be several days from now when the last of the hay was put up. It was sunny and looked to be warm. *A good day to be cutting hay*, thought Snyder. His mind went back to when he was a kid, just driving a team and mower round and round, daydreaming the whole time. In a way he was envious of Zack and his friends and what they had.

About mid-morning he arrived at the O'Keefe ranch. Mabel O'Keefe came out of the house in response to the barking dog and her boy Teddy, hollering, MaMa, MaMa, there's a man here."

The Sheriff reined his horse to a halt and motioned as if to doff his hat. "Mornin' Mrs. O'Keefe. I'm Sheriff Herb Snyder from Idaho City. I come to pay my respects. I was real sorry to hear about your husband."

At first, the same sad look that was quick to overtake Mabel whenever Harley's passing was mentioned came to her face, but then her eyes settled on Snyder's badge and her look became hateful. She said, sarcastically, "You should be."

Snyder was taken aback but not totally surprised by the widow O'Keefe's hostile response. It tended to add credence to how Shorty had been with him earlier that morning. He came back, his tone mindful of the woman's emotional state, "I know it's too late for yer husband, Ma'am, but my intention is to ask the U.S. Marshal down in Boise for some help. It's a big country."

Mabel's eyes had become teary, but she did not succumb to the urge to cry one more time. She said, somewhat bitter, "I wished you'd done that before now."

Snyder sighed. He wanted to say that he hadn't known about the rustling, but that wasn't true. He felt tongue-tied, like he was in a bad dream and helpless to do anything. Finally, he said, "How are ya gittin' along?"

It was now Mabel's turn to dodge the truth. "It's hard but we're getting by, we're getting by just fine. Harley hired a couple of fellows to build fence and such last summer. Those men take care of things day to day."

It came to Snyder that a widow woman with two young kids would be easy to take advantage of. He came back so as to not insult her judgement on the matter, "These boys are good hands, are they?"

"They are. They're moving the cattle to some open range down towards the Payette. Frank says its steep country but there's still plenty of graze left. You know Sheriff, with the way folks is fencing off the land these days, it makes easy grass hard to come by."

"I 'spect it does." Snyder paused and then allowed his suspicious side a freer rein, "Have you noticed any comings and goings here abouts as of late that seems peculiar to ya?"

Mabel smiled weakly like the Sheriff's question bordered on ridiculous. "I seldom leave the place. The last I recall going anywhere was this past spring, May I believe it was. Harley took us all in the wagon to Placerville. We got salt for the cattle and barbed wire and staples and flour and beans, and oh, I don't know what all, but just before we came home Harley treated us to a meal in town." And then she abruptly went silent as her voice had started to crack and her eyes were watering again. It was, apparently, too soon for her to be able to recall her life when Harley had been part of it.

Snyder looked away so as to allow Mabel time to compose herself. Seeing an opening in adult conversation, Teddy shouted out, "What's yer horses's name, Mister?"

"Boots," replied the Sheriff.

Teddy tilted his head back slightly and peered up at Snyder from beneath the brim of his black slouch hat. "Is that on account of her having white above all her hooves?"

"It is. I was gonna call her stockings but then I thought, well that's a dumb name."

Teddy scrunched his face up in a frown. "Yeah, I think it is too."

And then Mabel interrupted, "So, where are you off to Sheriff?"

"I thought it might be good to talk to yer hands since they're out in the hills. Maybe they've seen something or somebody that doesn't seem right to 'em."

"That could be, although neither has mentioned anything to me, but then I seldom see Gerald. He stays out mostly with the stock."

"Gerald?"

"Yes, Gerald Barnes."

"And Frank's last name?"

"Harper. He said they were going to put our cattle on some graze north of the Payette. Our brand is the slash Z on the left hip."

Snyder nodded. "I'm much obliged for the information, Ma'am. If I happen ta run into those boys it won't be like they're total strangers with somebody else's cattle. That's a good thing ta know in my job."

"Yes, I suppose it would be."

Snyder gathered his reins a little tighter as he lifted his hands from the pommel of his saddle where they had been resting. In parting, he thought to offer up his condolences again but, fearful she might throw it back at him, he stopped short of it. "Well Ma'am, I'm gonna move on. I'll likely be back by this way in a coupla days. If I've learnt anything new concernin' yer husband's situation, I'll stop in and share it with you."

"I would appreciate that, Sheriff."

Snyder made eye contact with the widow O'Keefe and touched his right hand to the brim of his hat before reining his horse around.

And then Teddy, a short string bean version of Harley, shouted out, "I hope you catch whoever it was that killed my pa."

The Sheriff waived feebly to the boy. "I'll try." And with that he nudged Boots into a trot so as to hasten his departure from their sorrow and the guilt that was taking root in his mind. He kept on at this gait until the road had entered the big pine trees and jogged to the left and out of their sight. Both he and Boots welcomed the slower pace causing her to jerk her head up and down a couple of times in resistance to the bridle before snorting heavily as if to clear her nostrils. Snyder looked around. It was timber covered mountains in all directions except to the north, toward the South Fork of the Payette River. The enormity and ruggedness of the country was intimidating, especially when he considered the task before him. *I've got ta catch these boys red-handed,* he said to himself, *or I'll be fouled. These people will still see me as a do-nuthin sheriff. I 'bout gotta bring'em a body draped across a saddle ta show'em they're wrong.* The perception that the widow O'Keefe and Shorty and Able held of him was unfair, to his way of thinking. It had created an anger within him, a desperation almost, to salvage his reputation that was in danger of clouding his judgement.

CHAPTER FOURTEEN

Sheriff Snyder had been gone three days from their place. During that time, Zack felt like he had redeemed himself somewhat in the eyes of Shorty and Able by cutting hay the first two days until it was too dark to see. But now, come the third day, he was finished with the mowing by ten o'clock in the morning. He was taking some pride in the fact that he alone had mowed all 30 acres of the meadow north of their home place. The soil there was dark and rich giving rise to a lush stand of bluegrass, brome and fescue. It had been soothing for him to listen to the raspy chatter of the sickle bar moving back and forth and back and forth as he circled the pasture laying the grass down. However, by the time he was done, the naysayer within him had become relentless in pointing out that this meadow they had worked so hard to fence last spring was the real gold claim, and not the piddling specks of yellow that he had found in the creek with the X on it.

Zack grunted as he lifted the cutter bar of the mower to an upright position and locked it in place for the trip back down the canyon to the house. He then climbed onto the mower's metal seat and rippled the reins over the backs of his two-horse team. "Giddup." The big Percherons did not hesitate as they lunged into their harnesses causing the mower to start with a jolt. It was close to three quarters of a mile from the hay meadow to the home place. Neither the two-track nor the steel wheels of the mower lent themselves to traveling very fast. For some reason, as the big work horses plodded along, Zack's thoughts went back to the day when he had encountered Katherine's father driving their team unmercifully up the pass towards Placerville. The images of that day caused him to sigh and shake his head. He said to himself, *I'll probably not be welcome in his store but I guess that won't matter if I ain't courtin' Katherine.* And then he snorted, just short of a laugh. *I go through all this and now Li Ming is gone to parts unknown. Just my luck.*

Zack drove the mower to a spot south of the corrals where they kept their farm equipment. He parked it next to the buck rake and began unhitching the horses when from behind him came Able's voice, his tone friendly, "Ya got 'er done did ya?"

Zack turned around. He supposed that Able and Shorty had been within their rights to treat him the way they had due to his going off to hunt for gold. But even now, after he'd *gotten his senses back,* as Shorty had put it, and things between them seemed to be on the mend, it still bothered him that they could turn on him so quick. It had caused him a nagging hurt that was not entirely gone, but it was more tolerable. He came back, "Yes sir, I do. We just need ah couple two-three days ah sunshine and we can put 'er in the stack."

Able turned his head to the side and spit some tobacco juice. "Yeah, sometimes gittin' mother nature to cooperate in such matters can be a tall order. But, I'm thinkin' we're 'bout due for some good luck." Able paused and then added, "While we're waitin' on the hay ta dry, it might be a good time for you to run into Idaho City and file on that gold claim up in the meadows." He spit again before laughing briefly. "Hell, that could be our retirement pension." And then he and Zack both laughed.

It felt good to Zack to share a laugh with Able, for things to be as they had before all the dissention due to the rustlers and Li Ming, but he was uncertain of where he stood with Shorty. He had no desire to sour his relationship with him now that it was coming back on track. He said, "There ain't but a handful a people, and one of 'em being Bickers, that knows about Toby Sing's gold strike, if you can call it that. So, I'm wonderin' if filing on it can't wait 'till we got the rest a the hay stacked?"

"It's yer call but I'm thinkin' now is a good time. Like I was tellin' ya last night when me an' Shorty come back from checkin' the stock. The calves is fat. Another three weeks, I figure, and we'll cut them off their mamas and trail 'em down ta Boise. And right after that we'll be gatherin' horses to break so's we can sell 'em to the Army. Come three weeks from now, we'll be busier than a one-armed man sittin' on a manure pile swattin' the flies away."

It seemed to Zack that Able had gone the extra mile to make his case as to why now was the best time for him to go file on the claim. To refuse to go, he sensed, would be akin almost to insulting Able's judgement on the matter. He came back, "I reckon I could slip on down there tomorrow and, if I don't tarry along the way, be back 'fore sundown the next day."

Able nodded. "Sounds workable to me."

"You should come along. Wet yer whistle in the big city."

A wry smile came to Able's face. "If I was ta do that it might prolong the trip."

Zack laughed. "I'll be there to keep you on the straight and narrow."

Able snorted and tossed his head back before refocusing on Zack. "I don't seem ta recall when that strategy has ever panned out."

Zack had a big grin on his face. "Well, maybe this'll be the time."

"We can talk about it later."

A kerosene chimney lantern sat in the center of the table. Its light defined the lazy swirls of the blue-white smoke that hung over the dirty dishes. Able sat at the far end of the table while Zack and Shorty sat across from one another. They had waited until the eating part of supper was over and the three of them, satiated on venison and fried spuds, were sipping a cup of coffee and having a roll your own cigarette. Able drew on his cigarette and then casually blew the smoke out before him like he didn't have a care in the world. Looking over at Shorty, he said, "I was thinkin' a ridin' on down to the city tomorrow with Zack ta file on that claim."

For just an instant, it appeared like Shorty either hadn't heard what Able had said, or he had and couldn't believe it. He shot back, "The hell you say."

Able was taken aback and not quite certain how to respond. He'd not yet formulated a response when Shorty snapped again, his voice filled with sarcasm.

"What, does it take two of ya ta hold the pen?"

Able was about to defend himself when Shorty barked again. "Yeah, the both ah you two hooligans, go on down there. Have yerselves a good time. Don't mind me, I'll just laugh myself silly building fence around the haystack in the lower pasture. Oh, and if I git bored with that I can always go up the canyon and cut a wagon load of firewood. Should be a grand time." And with that, Shorty slid his chair back from the table and got to his feet. He glanced over at Zack but then quickly settled into a hard stare at Able. "Yes sir, you two pups just have yerself a fine time."

Anger had come to Able's eyes. He fired back, "Ah to hell with it, Shorty. I'd forgot about fencing that stackyard."

"So you say."

"No, I did. I'll stay here and help ya."

"Hell no, I don't want yer help. You go ta town. Maybe you'll find Zack's Chinese whore along the way. Who knows, maybe you'll find one of yer own."

"There ain't no need ta git so fired up about this."

Shorty shook his head in disgust. "You boys go on ta town. Just leave the General dog here. He's better company than either one a you two anyway." And with that Shorty went outside, slamming the door behind him.

Able and Zack looked at one another, straight faced for a few seconds until suddenly, the both of them broke out in muffled laughter, like mischievous school boys that had just pulled off some prank. This went on for a good 20 or 30 seconds before they collected themselves. Able said, "Well, that didn't go quite as I thought it would."

"Unless you was thinkin' it'd be akin ta pokin' a hornet's nest with a sharp stick, I'd say you was way off." They laughed again, trying their best to keep it so Shorty wouldn't hear and then Zack went on, "Maybe we should just wait on the filing 'till Shorty is ok with it."

Able frowned. "Hell, there ain't never a time around here that there ain't somethin' that needs done. No sir, I'd rather make the trip now."

"Well," began Zack with some hesitation, "why don't we see what Shorty's mood is come tomorrow morning?"

An annoyed look came to Able's face. He sighed as if he didn't agree, but he said, "Alright, maybe sleepin' on it will change his mind, but I wouldn't bet on it."

CHAPTER FIFTEEN

They were nearing the fork in the road and the spot where Harley had been killed. Instinctively, both Zack and Able looked up to the ridgetop where the shooters had hidden themselves. For Zack, the sights and sounds of that morning were as fresh in his mind as if they'd happened only minutes ago. Even now, a shiver swept over him.

Sensing the somber chill that had come over them, Able said, "Yes sir, I was totally befuddled as to the change in Shorty's thinkin' this morning."

Zack looked away from the wooded ridge and glanced over at Able and grinned. "Well, what all was on that list ah wants that he gave you? Let me see now, there was Prince Albert and papers, a bottle of Old Crow, some new gloves, and, oh yeah, you don't want ta forget those gloves since like he said, he'll wear his out building fence and chopping wood." Zack then broke into a laugh.

Able was struggling to keep a straight face while pretending to be upset that Shorty had gotten the better of him when his focus went up the road to a wagon and team coming their way. He nodded towards it, "Ain't that Harley's widow?"

The wagon was still a good quarter mile away but coming at a steady clip. Zack recognized the horses, one a buckskin and the other a sorrel with a white star on its forehead. He said, "I reckon it is, that's Harley's team."

Able spit some tobacco juice to the side of his horse before saying. "She didn't make the turn to Placerville, so that kinda narrows it right down as to where she's goin'"

"Wonder what she wants?"

"I don't know, but my gut tells me it ain't gonna be good."

They went silent, urging their horses on towards the widow O'Keefe while speculating in their minds as to her reason for coming their way. In less than a minute, they were close enough to read the concern on her face. It was framed, accentuated by the yellow sunbonnet that covered her head. She braced her feet on the footrest of the wagon and pulled back hard on the reins. "Whoa team, whoa." The wagon came to a stop next to Zack and Able who were sitting on their horses at the edge of the road. Mabel's worry, whatever it was, had infected her daughter, Sarah, but not apparently Teddy, who was sitting in the back of the wagon blowing on a makeshift whistle.

Zack called out, as if he hadn't read her eyes, "Mornin' Ma'am, how are you this fine day?"

"I'm, well I'm not certain."

"Why's that?"

"Our hired man, Frank, he left four days ago to help Gerald move our cattle to better graze and he hasn't come back."

A surprised look came to Zack's face. "Are you talkin' about those cows and calves that was in the burn area near yer place?"

"Yes, that's the only bunch of cows we have. Frank said he wanted to move them so he could save the burn pasture for later this fall. He said he'd be back in a couple of days but it's been twice that long. I'm wondering if foul play has come his way, just like Harley."

"It does sound peculiar, Ma'am," said Zack in a fearful tone. "I take it this is contrary to his usual way a doin' things."

Mabel was about to speak when Teddy blew on his tinny, airy sounding whistle causing his mother to twist around in her seat. "Son, please don't do that while we're talking."

The image of the .44-100 shell casing that he had picked up on the ridge from which Harley's killer had fired was permanent in Zack's mind. In the brief moment that Mrs. O'Keefe had leaned back he could see between her and Sarah what it was that Teddy was blowing on. It caused him to blurt out, "Teddy can I look at that empty cartridge ya got there?"

Teddy went to the edge of the wagon and held the shell casing out. Zack knew before he looked at the numbers stamped on the head of it, what caliber it was. Nonetheless, he read what was imbedded in the brass, *.44-100*. He passed the empty shell over to Able, as he did, he asked Teddy, "Where'd you git this?"

Mabel cut in, "Why does it matter?"

Zack looked at her in a serious way. "It's likely the caliber of gun that killed Harley."

It appeared, just briefly, that Mabel might cave-in to her emotions, but then she caught herself and turned to Teddy. "Where did you find this?"

"Down in the burn," said Teddy in a halting voice.

"Did you see who fired the gun that left it there?" asked Able.

Teddy nodded. "It was Frank. He was shootin' at a coyote."

The boy had barely finished his declaration when Zack's mind went back to that day and Harley pitching out of his saddle and, in the next instant, getting shot himself. In the past, the shooter had been faceless, but now, he could see Frank, the cow milker, and Frank, the grave digger up on that ridge. And then the hired hand's fate came closer to being sealed. "Ma'am, do you recall where this fella was on the day Harley was killed?" asked Zack.

Anger flooded Mabel's face as she appeared to be sorting back through time. She was quiet, anguished for a moment until finally she said, "I can't say for sure. Harley told the men where to go and what to do."

"Mama," said Sarah, "Frank wasn't there at noon. I don't know where he went but he didn't come back 'till later in the day. It was well –" she paused, seemingly unable to say what came next and then a surge of emotion allowed her to finish, "it was after they brought daddy home."

"Oh my," said Mabel, "the Sheriff was inquiring about Frank and Gerald and where they might be. He seemed intent on looking them up."

Zack looked over at Able. "This don't sound good ta me."

"Maybe we ought ta see if we can locate Snyder 'fore he runs into this pair unawares of this Frank fella's credentials."

Zack shifted his attention to Mabel, whose eyes had gotten watery but were holding their own in contrast to her kids who were both sniffling and crying in a restrained way. He said, "Did the Sheriff say where he was going?"

"Up along the Payette. That's where I told him Frank was taking the cattle."

It occurred to Zack that Frank had probably lied to Mabel about his intentions, but he did not share this with her. He came back, "We'll make a swing up in that country an' see what we can turn up."

"You'll let me know what you find? We can't make it without those cattle."

Zack frowned and nodded his head. "We're all in that boat." He paused and then added, "Probably be a day or two 'fore we come back by."

Mabel shook her head. "I should've known those boys staying on to help a widow woman was too good to be true."

Although he didn't believe it himself, Zack said, to give her some hope, "All this business with the rifle could be pure coincidence. It might be things will turn out just fine."

Mabel looked at Zack and scoffed. "I'm a little too old for the tooth fairy, Mr. Kotter."

Zack glanced at Mabel, but then gestured with the empty cartridge to Teddy. "Ya mind if I keep this for a while?"

Teddy scrunched his face up so as to be hateful, "You can have it. I don't ever wanna see it again."

Zack nodded and tucked the shell casing into his shirt pocket next to his Bull Durham and papers. He said, "Ma'am, would ya like for us to escort you back home?"

"No thank-you. We should be ok unless these scalawags have taken to shooting women and kids. You boys be careful." And with that, the widow O'Keefe started the wagon on down the road in search of a good place to turn around.

Zack and Able rode on. By late morning they had reached the South Fork of the Payette. There had been ample evidence on the road, in the form of cow tracks and manure, that a small herd of cattle had been driven this way several days ago. But, as of yet, they had not seen the actual animals, nor the Sheriff. They'd just crossed the bridge spanning the river about 20 miles downstream from Lowman. The cow tracks, although even more diluted by the increased traffic, appeared to be headed west. "Where is it you reckon they're going to?" asked Able.

For a time, Zack did not interrupt the rhythmic creaking of his saddle's leather and the plodding steps of Biscuits in the powdery dirt of the road. Finally, he said, as if his answer had gelled sufficiently to be more credible, "I'm thinkin' these boys are intent on takin' Harley's whole herd clear outta the area where they'll be able to dummy up a bill of sale and sell'em. If they git far enough away there won't be anybody that recognizes Harley's brand and know what's gone on with him. That's what is in my crystal ball."

"You may be right. It's what I'd do if I was of a mind to steal somebody's cattle."

"My worry is that with a four day head start they could dispose of Harley's cattle 'fore we catch up to 'em."

Able turned his head and spit tobacco juice. Sensing that some of the juice had clung to his moustache, he ran the back of his left hand across his mouth. He came back, "I reckon I ain't gotta remind ya that we ain't got ah bean or ah biscuit between us and only our slickers to sleep on."

Zack looked over at Able and shook his head. "I guess we need ta pick up the pace."

It was about five miles downstream to where the Middle Fork of the Payette dumped into the South Fork. The canyon broadened out considerably here being close to a mile wide. To the south, timber covered mountains bordered it, while to the north, the ponderosa pine was scattered on the steep grassy slopes. It was here, Zack supposed, that Frank was bringing Harley's cattle, but none were in sight.

They had stopped just short of the bridge crossing the Middle Fork. About a quarter mile up the canyon to their right was a cabin. It appeared to have been there for quite some time as its logs had weathered to a grayish white. A man was standing in front of the cabin, staring back at Zack and Able who were both looking his direction. Able laughed. "I reckon it'd be bad manners to not go call on this fella now."

Zack smiled and nodded. "We might be well advised to talk to 'im anyway. I'd say the chances are good that he saw Frank and this Gerald guy go by here with Harley's cattle."

And then the man at the cabin raised his right arm and gave a big wave.

Able looked at Zack. "I guess that cinches it."

They started their horses on a well-defined wagon road that paralleled the Middle Fork. To either side of the road were sporadic patches of sagebrush within a carpet of grass that had begun to turn yellow. Between the cabin and the river, the old man had cleared the brush and grass and plant-ed a large garden. It was, Zack reckoned, close to an acre in size. There were rows of corn taller than a man and what appeared to be spuds and squash and carrots and other stuff that Zack was uncertain of. About a hundred feet beyond the cabin was an outhouse. Not far from it was the man's trash heap. The path leading to each showed years of use. To the east of the cabin was a pole corral and a small log barn with an oversize front door. The far side of the corral opened into a small pasture that had a barbed wire fence around it. Two mules, a white one and a sorrel colored one, both sleek and fat, were grazing there. *This old boy has got a little slice ah paradise*, said Zack to himself.

The owner of the cabin was small in stature, with short salt and pepper hair and a bushy moustache. He was dressed as one might expect a miner to be with a dingy brown cotton shirt, heavy denim pants that were being held up by red suspenders and a crumpled gray felt hat that was weathered and sweat-stained. He called out, "Afternoon to ya."

"Afternoon," said Zack. "Mind if we step down?"

The crow's feet gathered at the outer corners of the old man's dark eyes seemed to draw a little tighter as he said in a cordial tone, "Help yerselves. Got some breakfast coffee inside. Won't take but a minute ta heat it." And then, when their feet had barely hit the ground, the old man stepped towards them with his right hand out, "Name's Herman Selkirk."

Zack and then Able introduced themselves as they shook Herman's hand. He came back, "So where you fellas headed to?"

"We're lookin' for a coupla men trailing some cattle," said Zack. "The road down below shows sign that maybe a small bunch a cows has been over it recently. You wouldn't by chance have seen these go by, would ya?"

Herman chuckled. "Boy, ever body is lookin' for those cows."

"How's that?"

"A lawman from over ta Idaho City stopped by here. He wanted ta know the same thing. Said these cattle belonged to a widow woman back up the canyon and down towards Placerville somewhere."

"So, you saw the cattle come by here?" asked Able.

"Oh yeah," said the old man pointing to the main road along the South Fork like it was necessary for clarification. "There was maybe fifty, sixty of 'em, cows and calves. They stopped for a time down here in the sage flat and let 'em graze."

"There shudda been two men pushin' these cattle," said Zack. "You didn't happen ta talk to 'em did ya?"

"Two?" said Herman in a puzzled voice. "Maybe we're talkin' about a different bunch of cattle."

"Why's that?"

"Well, there was three men and a Chinese woman with these critters."

Zack's heart quickened as his thoughts went back to that day at Elk meadows when Bickers gloated as he told him that he'd never find Li Ming now. He said, with a hint of emotion in his voice, "This Chinese woman, what'd she look like?"

"Well sir, she was dressed like a man. She had an old black hat on but her hair was real long. She had it done up in a pigtail that hung way down her back. At first, I thought she was a boy on account of she was small and her face was smooth." Herman paused and then added, "She wasn't too bosomy either, especially in that shirt she was wearin'. It looked like it was a couple sizes too big for her."

"You didn't happen ta talk to her did ya?"

"No, the fella she was with did all the talkin'."

"What'd this fella look like?"

"Oh hell, I don't know," snorted Herman, "he was about yer size but older and he had a cookie duster, black like his hair."

"He didn't happen to give ya his name, did he?"

Herman was thoughtful for a moment and then he said, "Nope, he wasn't a real friendly type. Him and the girl rode up, he asked if I could spare some coffee and flour. I told him I was gittin' low my own self and couldn't part with any and he says alright and rides off. And that was it, they moved on."

Zack had come to the conclusion some time ago that Frank and whoever else was with him had stolen the widow O'Keefe's cattle. To hear now that they wouldn't rob an old man of his coffee and flour caused him to smile in a derisive way and shake his head in bewilderment. He said, "You remember anything else about this guy?"

A distant look came to Herman's face like he was recalling that day when suddenly he said, "Oh, this fella was ridin' a gray horse."

Zack and Able instantly looked at one another in a knowing way. Herman picked up on it. He said, "That mean somethin' ta you boys?"

Able came back, "A rustler in these parts has been known to ride a gray horse."

"Well, that musta been why the sheriff was inquirin' about these boys too."

"When was it the sheriff was by here?" asked Zack.

"Day before yesterday, about noon I think it was."

"He happen ta say anything about his intentions after he left yer place?"

"No, but I watched him turn on down the crik. I reckon he was gonna try and catch up to those folks, but I could see it in his face from the second I told him about the fella on the gray horse that he was nervous about it. I wouldn't go so far as to say he was afraid, but it was close to it."

"A prudent man might show some fear," said Zack. "And that's ok by me if he still does his job."

Silence overtook Herman, who thus far had been given to loquacity. It was followed by a sheepish look and then he said, "I forgot to mention that sometime after the sheriff left, I heard a coupla gunshots way off down the canyon."

Zack allowed the possibility of what the gunshots might mean to fester in the space between him and Herman until finally he gave the old man a reprieve from going there. He said, looking at Able, "Ya reckon we oughta move on?"

"I suppose so."

To Herman, Zack said, "Thanks for the information."

"Good luck with findin' them cows."

Zack nodded towards the old man and then he and Able got on their horses and rode off at a good clip. They had gone back down along the stream that ran past Herman's cabin to the wooden bridge and crossed over it before either of them spoke, Able said, "I don't believe I care for the odds that Snyder was facin'."

"Nor do I," said Zack, "Just two shots with four men involved, it don't sound good for the Sheriff."

"Maybe it was just somebody gittin' themselves some venison."

Zack looked over at Able. His face read like a book. It was clear that he didn't really believe what he'd just said but before Zack could comment on it, Able moved on, "You reckon that's Li Ming with this fella on the gray horse?"

"I wouldn't bet against it." As much as he'd wanted to help Li Ming, Zack had just about convinced himself that she was gone and that he could, in good conscience, tend to business on their ranch. But now, those old feelings were taking hold of him again. He added, "I'm thinkin' this gray horse guy is the poker player that beat Bickers outta Li Ming."

Able hesitated momentarily as he tried to gauge where Zack stood on the matter of Li Ming and then he said, "It would appear that this gray horse fella ain't gonna put her ta whorin', at least not yet anyway."

"He's a thief and a scoundrel. At some point, after he settles in somewhere, my thinkin' is he'll put her back to it."

"You thinkin' ta git her away from him?"

"I reckon so, but gittin' Harley's cattle back comes first."

A wry smile came to Able's face. "You likely ain't gonna git one without the other."

"Probably not."

They rode on, mostly in silence, each with his own speculation as to what lay ahead when off to their right a hint of what they had feared showed itself in the form of a coyote. Zack reined Biscuits to a halt and watched as the coyote ran into the timber. Within seconds, several ravens flew out from the trees, cackling angrily. And then a cacophony of protests from the ravens and Steller's jays still within the thicket erupted. Zack looked over at Able. He thought to make some benign comment like, *probably just a gut pile from a deer that somebody shot.* But he knew that would only make the disappointment if he was wrong even worse. He sighed. "Guess we better have a look see."

It was about a hundred yards through knee-high sage and grass to get where all of the racket was coming from. Reluctantly, Zack started through it allowing Biscuits to pick his own way. Able followed close behind. When they were close enough to hear the coyote growling and snapping at the birds, they dismounted, neither saying a word but drawing their pistols, nonetheless. In the back of their minds, common sense told them it was unnecessary but the aura of death and evil was too strong to ignore the impulse to arm themselves. They proceeded on foot, being especially careful to not step on anything that would make noise. A gentle breeze suddenly assaulted their senses with the rank, nauseous smell of death. And then through a sliver of daylight in the morass of green limbs, Zack caught glimpses of movement. It caused him to freeze in his tracks. It was a kaleidoscope of brown fur, black feathers and then pearly white. Instantly, his mind went back to the bluffs above the Little Bighorn and the last time he'd seen that texture of white. His heart began to hammer even harder as he stepped towards the opening in the trees. The coyote was the first to bolt followed by an upward explosion of ravens, but not all of them, some having the audacity to simply hop a short distance away. Zack's eyes darted here and there, looking for bigger scavengers. Satisfied there were none, he came back to the white, the exposed, fleshless ribs of a man. The sudden realization of what he was looking at caused a painful adrenaline surge within him. Saying nothing, he looked over at Able who grimaced slightly and shook his head. They both knew who it was the ribs likely belonged to. Zack looked back at the partially exposed rib cage and started forward when abruptly, from the corner of his left eye, he caught sight of something that made him jump to the side. There, beneath a sagebrush plant was a hand and part of a forearm with shreds of green cloth hanging from it. He said aloud, "Damned coyotes, they ain't got no respect for the dead." Zack took a breath to settle himself before looking down at the hand. It had a gold wedding band. Uncertain, he called out to Able, "Was the Sheriff married?"

Able, who was a short distance away, came back solemnly, "Yeah, he's got a wife and two kids. For a time, the other night, he went on about how he wanted ta do better by them and git 'em outta Idaho City. Maybe do somethin' besides be a lawman."

It had come to Zack, not long after Herman had told them there were three men with the cattle, that Snyder was not the slacker he'd once thought him to be. It seemed now so wrong to have thought that. Staring at the hand and the ring conjured up images in Zack's mind of Snyder's widow and her grief, even though he'd never met her. He moved on, before the guilt within him took over his conscience. The stench in the air was strong. It caused Zack to take short breaths and breathe in through his mouth. And then, right there in a patch of snowberry bushes, was definitive proof that Sheriff Herb Snyder had done his job and it had cost him his life. Zack and Able both contorted their faces commensurate to the horrific dismemberment of the Sheriff.

Able looked down at Snyder's upper torso. It was missing the right arm and left leg. Most of the flesh had been gnawed and pecked from the bones. Empty holes remained where the eyes had once been. Flies, big and black and bloated by the feast, swarmed over the remains. And the ants, hundreds of them, more deliberate in their feeding crawled in and out and over anyplace that might provide them sustenance. Able said, turning away, "Oh shit, Zack. This is nasty."

Zack forced himself to say, "You know we got ta bury him."

Able nodded. "You ever wonder why those got ta do things in life is generally the hardest."

For a moment, Zack's thoughts drifted to some of those *got ta do* times in his life, Toby Sing, Custer's men and now the Sheriff. He said, not to one-up Able, "I reckon, but for the grace ah God it could be our bones scattered about."

Able came back, not meaning to be overly smart-alecky but he was, "You know, since people seem to turn up dead around us, maybe we should start carrying a shovel."

It wasn't just the gruesomeness of the Sheriff's death, it was everything that had happened over the past couple of weeks that tempered Zack's response, "I'm thinkin' maybe we ought to go back ta Herman's and git shovels so we can give the Sheriff a decent burial. Maybe while we're there we can take him up on his hospitality."

And so, they left the unpleasantness of what remained of Sheriff Herb Snyder. In less than an hour they were back at the old man's cabin drinking coffee, trying to wash the taste of death from their mouths and smoking Bull Durham cigarettes in hopes of expunging the smell of decomposing flesh from their nostrils. They savored being away from the pine thicket where Herb Snyder lay, as tomorrow, they would be back there gathering his bones and putting them in a hole.

CHAPTER SIXTEEN

As they had expected, Herman invited them to spend the night at his place as it was too late to go back and dig the Sheriff's grave, at least in the daylight it was. Herman was not surprised at the news the Sheriff was dead and that vermin had ripped his body apart. He'd said, *There is some vile sons-ah-bitches in these parts. Killin' don't mean nuthin to 'em.* And then it seemed the three of them avoided talking about Herb Snyder's death and what awaited them tomorrow. There was nothing they could say that would bring him back, but there was plenty they could say that would allow him into the old man's cabin and their dreams that night.

The sun was still just an orange glow beyond the mountains off to the east when they started out the next morning. Frost covered the ground and gave all of the vegetation a white sparkly appearance. Their breathes, both men and horses, puffed out into the air before them. Herman stated the obvious, "Boys, she's cold enough ta freeze the balls off ah brass monkey."

Zack and Able laughed politely before Able came back, "Well, I guess its ah good thing we ain't brass monkeys."

And then they all laughed, maybe more than was warranted by their feeble attempts at humor but it kept at bay what lay ahead. Each of them had a shovel tied on behind the seat of his saddle. It was a task they would share unless Herman offered to bury the Sheriff by himself so that Zack and Able could catch up to the killers, but so far, he'd not done that.

Although they had not pushed the horses in the biting cold of the early morning, the trip to the thicket seemed much quicker than yesterday. Zack stopped Biscuits just short of where the trees got thick and dismounted. He said, as he began untying his shovel, "I reckon we can leave the horses in this clearing. There's a little graze here."

"And some sunshine," said Able sarcastically as he looked to the shadows cast by the tall pine trees where they would be digging the Sheriff's grave.

Zack looked over Biscuits' back and grinned. "Maybe you should just pretend its July."

"Well, maybe we both should and you can go take a dip in the river." And then they, minus Herman, forced themselves to laugh before entering the thicket. Zack led, followed by Able and then Herman. They were serious now.

Zack knew better than anybody where the Sheriff's hand with the ring was located. It was a grisly sight, but no more than the rest. He made no attempt to avoid it and let Able or Herman be first to stumble upon it. Instead, he went straight to it and picked it up as if it were delicate with feelings. From the corner of his eye he saw Herman cringe and turn away. To Able he said, "I reckon his wife would want the ring, don't ya think?"

Able nodded. "I 'spect she would."

Zack began pulling and twisting on the ring until finally it came off. He then tucked it deep into his pants pocket. He said, in a somber tone, "We'll git this to her when this is all said and done."

Able snorted. "You know, the hell of it is she ain't gonna have no idy where her husband is buried unless one of us brings her here. I ain't sayin' I got a problem with doin' that, it's just Herb's out here all by his lonesome."

Zack shook his head. "I reckon he's not the first good man to be buried that way."

"Let's just git on with it," said Herman with some edge in his voice.

Zack and Able both looked over at the old man. His eyes were reflections of the angst within him, but there was no graceful way to withdraw now. They went on towards where the bulk of Herb Snyder lay. And then they were there. During the night, the coyotes had returned, severing the Sheriff's head from his torso. It lay not far away, staring back at them. Within seconds, Herman began retching, spewing his breakfast in a steamy mass upon some sagebrush in front of him. The intensity of it brought him to his knees. Stringy globs of spittle hung from his mouth. Save for the ubiquitous ravens and Steller's jays, silence enveloped them until he retched again, except more deeply as he exhausted the contents of his stomach. And then his shame turned to anger, "You boys can go screw yerselves. I'm done with this."

They remained silent as the old man brushed his coat sleeve across his face and got to his feet. He stood there, staring at them through watery eyes that were struggling to salvage some dignity from what had just happened until finally, Zack said, "It's alright, Herman. I've seen good fighting men that's had their stomach's turned by sights like this."

A hint of relief came to the old man's eyes. He measured it back in contrition, "I'm sorry fellas. It just ain't in me ta do this."

"That's ok," said Able.

"Go on home, Herman," said Zack, "we'll leave yer shovels under some brush down near the road."

"Oh yeah, yeah, that'd be fine. You boys are welcome ta use 'em." He started to go but then looked back, being careful to keep his eyes elevated from the Sheriff's remains on the ground, "I'm sorry boys, I'm just real sorry."

It wasn't until they'd heard the old man get on his horse that Able said, "You know he ain't likely to forget this day anytime soon."

Zack sighed. "I hope he can. There ain't no good reason why a man should have ta deal with things like this other than the wickedness of other men." And then he offered, "If you wanna start diggin', I'll collect the rest of the Sheriff's bones."

Able protested weakly. "Ya sure? I'll help ya."

Zack shook his head and began walking away, towards the Sheriff's skull. He called out over his shoulder, "I'm ok with it." In reality, he was far from being ok with gathering the bones, but somebody had to do it and live with that experience. It would be his last payment for having left the work to Able and Shorty while he chased after Toby Sing's gold and Li Ming's freedom. He stopped, looking directly down on the head. Suddenly, it came to life in his mind, talking, laughing, unaware that this is how it would end up. Zack bent over and grasped it in his gloved hands, making sure the eye sockets looked away. No sooner had he done this than his offer to show Sam Wo where Toby Sing was buried echoed in his mind. It was their custom to exhume those that wanted to be buried in their homeland, clean their bones and put them in a metal box much smaller than a coffin and ship them back to their village in China. *I'll show him the way*, said Zack to himself, *but I ain't handling no more bones.*

It was close to noon when they had finished burying the Sheriff's remains. Zack had found a piece of shale rock and used the lead end of a rifle cartridge to scratch an inscription on it:

Sheriff Herb Snyder
Murdered by Rustlers
October 7, 1883

They had picked up their shovels and were about to leave when Able said, "Ya reckon we oughta say some words?"

Zack had never known Able to be one to talk to God but he generally thought it was a good thing if someone else did the talking. Zack came back, "I took the Sheriff to be the kind that would want it, someone that would give him a recommend to the almighty."

"Yes sir, a favorable sendoff," said Able.

Zack removed his hat and bowed his head. Able followed suit. Zack began, "Lord, We're sendin' a good man yer way ta-day. His name is Herb Snyder. He was kilt by thieves and murderers while trying ta recover a widow woman's property. We're hopin' you got a special place for him. He didn't deserve what has come his way. Thanks, Lord. Amen.

"Amen," whispered Able.

They hid the shovels, as they said they would, in the brush at the edge of the road and moved on. It couldn't be helped, those premonitions of ending up like the Sheriff if they continued on after the man on the gray horse and his friends. But on they went, it was the right thing to do. And then there was the matter of Li Ming. Zack knew now that there'd be no buying her back. It would not be necessary as the man in possession of her would either go to jail or die.

CHAPTER SEVENTEEN

For the last hour, they had been making their way by the light of the moon. It was full and bright, so much so that it made the brilliance of the millions of stars surrounding it inconsequential. It had not been their intention to travel after dark, but tending to the Sheriff had cost them valuable time. Their goal had been to reach Horseshoe Bend, which was about 25 miles on down the Payette River, by dusk, but that didn't happen. A loose collection of mostly log buildings to either side of the road they were on defined the town. A horse walking at a normal pace would be through it in a minute or less. Signs of life were scarce except for the Mint Saloon. Light shone from the four pane windows to either side of its front door. Directly above these windows, on the second floor, were another set of portals, evenly spaced to accommodate the rooms there. They were dark but looked out onto the two horses tied to the hitching rail below.

Able looked ahead of them. A smattering of pale, yellow light and blue smoke emanated from a few of the buildings but overall it was not inviting. Looking at the Mint, he said, "Ya reckon they got anything ta eat in there? I'm so hungry I could eat the bark off a tree."

Zack grinned, it being visible in the moonlight, "I suspect if they ain't got nuthin ta eat they got somethin' that'll make ya forget about wantin' to."

Able laughed but did not stop his horse knowing what their first order of business would be. He came back, "Ya reckon that livery man will be up and about?"

"Well, if he ain't, I guess he soon will be."

They rode on to the edge of town and an old barn-like structure on the river side of the road. A crudely painted sign with badly faded black letters about a foot tall on a white background hung above two big double doors at the front of the building. The sign read: LIVERY. Attached to the south side of the barn was a pole corral adjacent to a small pasture. The pasture was enclosed by a barbed wire fence that ran down to the Payette river so as to afford the animals confined there, water. The big double doors at the front of the building were closed, but a window to the left of them showed light. Zack got down from Biscuits and went over to the window and looked in. A slender, middle-aged man with short, but disheveled red hair, and a bushy moustache was lying on a narrow bed reading a dime western novel. A chimney lantern sitting on a nightstand next to the bed provided light. The man was wearing dark cotton pants and blue Union Jack underwear with gray socks that had holes in the toes. Zack tapped on the window while hollering, "Hello in there."

The livery man was caught totally unaware and jumped to his feet facing the window. Zack's face was distorted and shimmery in the poor light, regardless, the startled man shouted back. "What the hell do you want? You some kinda peepin Tom?"

Zack came back, "We got horses that need cared for."

The man frowned and then sighed as if to shed some of his anger. He waved Zack away from the window. "Give me a minute. I gotta git dressed." The man sat on the edge of his bed and began pulling his boots on, mumbling as he did, "These damned people think they can come in here all hours of the night. I'll tell ya, the things I gotta put up with just ta make a livin'...."

In the moonlight, Zack and Able started unsaddling their horses. Off in the distance, further downriver, they became aware of bawling calves. "Sounds like somebody is weanin' their calves," said Able.

Zack paused and cocked his ear in that direction. He listened for a moment. "Don't sound like there's a whole lot of 'em."

Able laughed. "I suspect people close by is glad ah that. You know how it is when you take those little rascals away from their mama. They'll bawl for two or three days."

"Yeah," grunted Zack as he pulled his saddle from Biscuits back, "they can be real troublesome if a fella is tryin' ta sleep anywhere near 'em."

From behind them, the barn doors creaked open. Zack and Able turned around. Zack called out. "Sorry ta roust ya out at this hour of the day."

"It ain't day," snorted the livery man, "the damned sun set a long time ago."

Zack purposely erased any sign of contrition from his face. "We'll be needin' some oats for our horses."

"That'll be two bits each, in advance."

Zack dug in his pocket and handed over the money. "We'll be needin' a coupla brushes too."

"Don't you fools know its late and its dark?"

Zack shot the man a look of disgust and shook his head. He said sarcastically, "I assume there's no charge to put our saddles inside?"

At last, some shame for how he was being came to the man's face. He said, as if to excuse his behavior, "Those damned calves over yonder kept me awake last night. I don't do well on short sleep."

"How long they been penned up?" asked Able.

"Coupla days. Some fellas came through with a little bunch a cows and calves and sold the calves to this guy next ta me."

Zack and Able exchanged knowing glances. Zack asked, "These boys have a Chinese woman with 'em?"

A surprised look came to the livery man's face. "They did." And then he snickered. "Some ole boy that was here then and seen 'em go through said that Chinese gal was a sportin' woman over at Idaho City. He said she was an unpleasant woman and damned sure not worth three dollars. Can ya believe it, three dollars for a roll in the hay? Why –"

Zack cut the man off. "These folks happen ta say where they were headed to?"

"I never talked to 'em but they kept on to the West, so I 'm wonderin' if they was headed to Oregon. Lots a cattle country south a Burns."

It was, as the crow flies, about 40 miles west to the Snake River, which marked the boundary between the Idaho Territory and the state of Oregon. The Snake was a large, deep river and not to be taken lightly. Zack came back, "You know of any reliable ferries crossin' the Snake?"

"South ah Payette, right there where the Malheur dumps into the Snake is one that lots ah folks use."

Zack was about to speak when Able cut him off, "Where'd you git that horse?"

The livery man was hesitant to look in the direction Able was pointing. A horse had wandered up from the pasture and was standing just beyond the corral. In the light of the moon, its white stocking feet were clearly visible. Zack chimed in, "That's Boots."

"You know that horse?" asked the livery man.

"Yeah, and I'm thinkin' you do too," said Zack in an angry tone. "I thought you said that you didn't talk to these people with the stolen cattle?"

"Stolen?"

"Don't play dumb, Mister. It won't do ya no good."

"I ain't. I'm tellin' ya straight, I bought this horse and a big black mule off a stranger that was passin' through "

"When was this?"

"Coupla days ago."

"What'd the guy look like?"

The livery man had become fearful and flustered in his demeanor, he said, his voice shaking, "I don't recall."

Zack scoffed. "Like hell you don't. You better tell it like it is now or we'll head on down ta Boise in the mornin' and pay a visit to that U.S. Marshal they got there."

A sudden spark of defiance came to the man. "You can drag me down there, but I got a bill of sale."

"Let's see it," said Able.

"It's inside."

"Well, let's go look at it," said Zack.

The livery man frowned and shook his head. "You boys got no right treatin' me like ya are," he said as he started towards the barn doors. "I'm an honest businessman."

Zack scoffed. "To my way ah thinkin', lyin' ain't got no part a honesty and we already caught ya in a lie."

The livery owner went silent as he walked into the near darkness of the barn. "It's in my living quarters," he said as he opened a door off to his left. Zack and Able followed him inside the small room. A stove with a coffee pot sitting on it was directly in front of them and to the right of the night stand. Across the room from the bed was a table with two wooden chairs. A heavy tan colored ceramic coffee mug along with salt and pepper shakers and a sugar bowl were on the table. But more importantly, on the shelf above the table, tucked in next to some cans of tomatoes, was a double action Smith & Wesson pistol. Zack's eyes locked on to it as the man retrieved a folded piece of paper from the nightstand. He opened it and began to read, "I, Bob Smith, do –"

Zack cut him off. "Was this Smith fella ridin' a gray horse?"

"I don't –"

"Yer memory better improve real quick, Mister, or I promise ya, you'll spend the night hog-tied and come mornin' we'll tie ya to yer saddle, if need be, and head fer Boise if you don't start tellin' the truth." And then Zack reached for the pistol on the shelf. "This gun," he said holding it up for the livery man and Able to see, "did you git this from the same man that sold you the horse and mule?"

The man sighed and nodded his head. He said, his voice barely above a whisper, "Yeah."

To Able, Zack said, "I'd bet money this is the Sheriff's pistol."

"Sheriff," blurted out the livery man. "This fella didn't say nuthin 'bout this gun belonging to a lawman."

"You fool," said Able angrily, "the horse and mule do too."

Zack piled on, "And his saddle, rifle, pack saddle, all his gear, did ya git that too? Just where in hell did you think this Smith fella got all this stuff?"

Fearful desperation gripped the man's face. He shook his head. "He said they'd come across a fella out in the mountains that was sick and they did what they could for him but he died during the night. He said the guy had told them they could have his belongings if he didn't make it."

Able laughed derisively. "Do you believe in Santa Claus too?"

"Alright, Mister," said Zack sternly, "time ta fess up. Did this fella tell ya where him and his friends were headed?"

"Not straight out, he didn't. He asked directions to that same ferry I told you about."

"And nothing else?"

"He wasn't a real sociable guy."

Out of the blue, Zack came back, "How was it between this Smith fella and the Chinese girl?"

Able glanced over at Zack, but then shifted his attention back to the stable owner.

"Whaddaya mean?" asked the livery man.

"How was he treatin' her?"

A slightly puzzled look came to the livery man's face. He shrugged, "Ok, as far as I could see."

For a moment Zack pondered all that he'd heard, finally he said, "You know, yer dealin' in stolen property and yer neighbor too that bought those calves. My advice to you is to hang on to it till the marshal in Boise can sort it out."

"But, I didn't know all this was stolen."

Zack grinned. "Maybe you can convince the marshal of that."

CHAPTER EIGHTEEN

As it turned out, the Mint was the only place in town to get anything to eat or a bed for the night. The fare was nothing fancy, beans and sourdough biscuits and warm beer, but for a couple of ex-cavalry soldiers who'd been accustomed to far less at times, it suited them just fine. Their rooms, however, were a different story. Up until about a month ago the Mint had offered the services of sporting women. Cleanliness had not been a priority. The rooms reeked of cigar and cigarette smoke. The beds smelled of sweat, liquor and sex. The rough plank floor was stained with tobacco juice, vomit and more spilled liquor. And the log walls were plain and boring and bare, except for a Boise Mercantile calendar in Zack's room and a painting of some sunflowers in a vase surrounded by nothingness in Able's. The top part of the calendar depicted a peaceful mountain scene. It was on the wall opposite the foot of the bed. Zack wondered if that picture had been a distraction, a getaway fantasy for the girls, who, for a price, entertained anybody and everybody. Neither Zack nor Able undressed. They lay on top of the covers. The window in Zack's room was positioned such that it allowed the moonlight to illuminate the calendar scene. There were snow-capped peaks above a grassy mountain meadow with red and yellow and blue wildflowers. A bald eagle soared overhead. It was all so pure and wholesome. And then Zack's thoughts were invaded by Li Ming. He could see her in the room, on the bed, working and working and then, in the next instant, she was there, walking in the meadow, smiling and happy. And so went the night.

In the morning, after a breakfast of bacon, eggs, sourdough hotcakes and coffee that was surprisingly not bad, they headed out of town. As they neared the man's place who had bought the widow O'Keefe's calves, Able said, "Maybe we should just go on in ta Boise and put all this on that Marshal?"

Zack was quiet for a time, perhaps because he knew Able was right, but then he came back, "This bunch has already got a good lead on us. I'm afraid if we was ta go dilly-dallying in Boise ta git this Marshal, if he's even there, we'll end up losin' these scoundrels."

Able sighed his frustration, not caring mostly that Zack had observed it. "Ya know, if we strike out in ta that Oregon country, we ain't equipped ta camp along the way."

"There's ranches in that country. I reckon there'll be some that'll put us up for the night."

"Well, ya know, we're going on day three now. Shorty's gonna be wonderin' what happened to us."

Zack reined Biscuits to a stop and looked over at Able. "I got no problem going on by myself."

Able was quick to come back. "Oh hell no. I'll go along it's- "

"It might make some sense if you was ta go fetch the Marshal and have him come git Harley's calves back."

"Maybe we should both go for the Marshal. Maybe he could telegraph the law over in Oregon and have them be on the lookout for this bunch."

"We're close to these scalawags. From what I hear, that country south a Burns is big and not many folks out there. Plenty a places ta hide a little bunch a cows, and once they're hid there ain't no tellin' if a person 'll ever find 'em."

Able went silent, but it was clear he was like the proverbial pot about to boil over, and then he did, "Dammit Zack,

I'm thinkin' the reason yer doggin' these people's trail ain't due to Harley's cows, it's cuz you wanna catch up ta this Chinese girl. I mean, hells-bells, we've gave this an honest effort. We've found the Sheriff's stuff and Harley's calves. It's time ta turn this over to the law. We got our own ranch ta tend to, ya know."

Zack was taken aback, his tone became sober, "There's some truth in what you say. I can't explain it but I'm taken with Li Ming."

"It sounds ta me like she's free a whorin'."

"For now, maybe, but whose ta say on down the road."

"Well hell, since when is it yer job ta make her life better."

"She trusted me with Toby's gold claim. She's countin' on me."

Able laughed. "I'll bet she is, and if you was ta quit the ranch and go up ta that claim and work it for the next ten years you might be able ta buy her freedom."

"The way I see it, it's only a matter of time, and if the fella that's got her now don't change his ways, he ain't gonna be around."

"Well, there ya go. All you gotta do is let the law take care a this fella and you'll have yer girl."

Zack looked away and shook his head. "I'm gonna go on, Able. I don't want ta trust things ta chance. I'd appreciate it if you'd just go for the Marshal and after that go on home and help Shorty with the rest of the hay."

It was like Able had known all along that Zack wouldn't change his mind and this would be his position on the matter as he didn't appear to even think about it, he just spit it out, "Two days Zack, and then I'm going home. I'll go by way of Boise and Idaho City. I'll let the law know what's going on if we don't catch up to these folks."

Zack nodded. "I'll owe ya a sarsaparilla for this."

Able laughed. "You damn sure will."

CHAPTER NINETEEN

They followed the Payette River west to where it dumped into the Snake and the Washoe Ferry was located. The journey, being close to 50 miles, had taken the better part of two days causing them to spend the night in a road house along the way. They'd not left Horseshoe Bend on good terms with either of the people that had dealt with the thieves. The new owner of Harley's calves, when told they did not rightfully belong to him in spite of having a bill of sale from Bob Smith, was not happy. Zack told him that they intended to report the man's transaction to the marshal in Boise to which the man had replied, *That's fine and dandy. You just tell that sonovabitch ta bring me eight hundert an' twenty dollars and I'll help him gather 'em and push 'em out the gate, but if he ain't got cash money he'd be well advised ta not come around here or there'll be bad trouble. You tell 'im that.*

To which Zack had replied, *these calves belong to a friend of ours that was murdered. His widow and kids was countin' on sellin' 'em so as ta be able ta live this winter.*

The man laughed, *my wife and kids is fond ah eatin' too. Just a nasty habit they've picked up, I reckon.*

It was mid-afternoon when they arrived at the ferry. A scruffy, unkempt man of medium build rose up from a stump at the edge of the trees where he had been sitting. He called out, "You boys lookin' ta cross the river?"

Zack looked down at the man. He was wearing a black derby hat that was ineffective against the afternoon sun causing him to squint and shade his eyes with his right hand. Zack said, "We are."

"Cost ya two bits ah piece – on this side ah the river."

Zack smiled. "You git folks that wanna ride off without paying, do ya?"

The ferry man spit tobacco juice in a defiant manner towards the edge of the river and then he looked back at Zack and Able and shook his head as if he couldn't believe what he was about to say, "I had some jaspers in here yesterday with a bunch ah cows that was not wantin' ta pay until they was all on the other side. We damned near come ta fisticuffs over it."

From the corner of his eye, Zack could see Able look at him and then turn away. They'd talked earlier today on how tonight would be his last night before he would go to Boise and then home. But now, it was like they'd just come across some really fresh tracks. Zack said to the ferry operator, "This bunch ah cattle, there wasn't by chance a man ridin' a gray horse with a Chinese woman in tow with 'em was there? They probably had a coupla other guys with 'em too."

The man looked more intently, as if suspicious of Zack and Able, and then he said, "You boys the law?"

Able cut in, "No sir, but they're likely ta be here soon."

"Why's that?"

"These boys is thieves and killers," said Zack in a stern voice. "We been trailin' 'em for a good while now. Yer lucky they didn't just help themselves to yer ferry and be on their way."

The ferry operator, a middle-aged man with the beginnings of a salt and pepper beard, touched his hand to the pistol that rode high on his right hip. Zack recognized it as a Remington, Model 1875 in 44-40 caliber, a somewhat cumbersome gun. The ferry man said, his voice filled with obvious braggadocio, "Well, I'll tell ya there'd be no sure money on that proposition."

"So they paid ya?"

"They damned sure did. I had ta make eight trips to get them and the cows and their horses across." The ferry man laughed. "Those huckleberries had some ole boy waitin' on the other side to take possession of them cows. They tried ta put the bite on him for the ferry costs, but he wouldn't stand for it."

"Do you know who this guy was?"

"The ferry man came back quick, too quick, his tone evasive, "Nope, never seen 'im before."

Zack nodded, even though he was certain the man was lying. He moved on, "What about the others, the ones that brought the cattle, ya got any idy where they might have gone to?"

The man laughed. "Those two is sleepin' off a drunk at an inn a coupla miles down the road. I heard that from a fella that came through here 'bout an hour 'fore you two showed up."

Able caught Zack's eye. "That sounds like what those hands of Mrs. O'Keefe's would do. They're flush with their share of all the money they got for her cattle, so they celebrate last night."

Zack snorted. "I suspect they figure that since they killed the Sheriff and Harley, there's no one to come after 'em."

"These fellas killed a lawman?" asked the ferry man in a nervous tone.

"And the owner of the cattle you ferried," said Zack, "so, I'd be obliged if you'd git us across the river."

"Sure Mister, git on board."

The road on the Oregon side of the river forked three ways. To the left or south was toward the Owyhee River country, to the west was Burns and to the north was Umatilla and the Columbia River. It was obvious the cattle had been driven south. "Which way to this inn," asked Zack.

"Thataway, ah coupla miles," said the ferry man as he pointed to the road going north.

"Much obliged," said Zack.

The ferry man, seeing a new customer on the other side of the river, hollered out, "Good luck to you boys," and then he jabbed his long pole into the water and shoved off, sliding along the heavy cable that held his big raft in place as he went across the river.

From his saddle, Able was first to broach their dilemma, "Ya know, now that these scoundrels ain't in possession of Harley's cattle they could claim they're just innocent folks, mindin' their own business."

Zack sighed and spit some tobacco juice off the other side of Biscuits. "And if we chase this fellar down that bought the cattle we'll be back in that same pissin' contest we was in with the fella that bought the calves and his bogus bill of sale from Bob Smith." Zack shook his head in disgust. "My vote is we go git Missus O'Keefe's money."

Able snorted and tossed his head back. "You know, to an outsider comin' along it could look like we was just robbin' ah coupla law-abidin' citizens."

"Well, I reckon it ain't the first time that decent folks has had to become vigilantes to set things right."

They rode on at a gallop, up the north fork towards the inn and what awaited them there. For the most part, the road paralleled the river and its cloak of cottonwoods and willow that quickly gave way to sagebrush and scattered juniper on the west side of the road. Within minutes, they were in sight of a single-story log shack with a dirt roof that was set back in the cottonwood trees. Blue smoke that rolled from its rusty stovepipe showed the only evidence of life. *They must be startin' ta cook their supper*, said Zack to himself as he slowed Biscuits to a walk before guiding him off the road and into the trees. Able followed him. Yellow leaves littered the ground making a crunching sound beneath the horses' hooves. They dismounted about a hundred yards short of the inn and led the horses further into the woods where they were totally hidden and tied them off.

Zack's heart was pounding hard in anticipation of what they had to do, he said, "I reckon these boys is gonna be purty sassy, that Frank fella struck me that way."

Able's eyes were wide and excited looking, he said as he took a short breath to steady himself, "The way I see it, we need ta surprise these fellas, just throw down on 'em when they ain't expectin' it. So, maybe we wait till they come out."

Zack came back quick, as if he'd already pondered Able's strategy and found the flaw in it, "That'd be alright, except we don't know what Gerald looks like. He could come out and ride off and we'd be just sittin' there thinkin' we still got the both of 'em cornered inside."

Able snorted. "Well, who's ta say they ain't already left. I didn't see no horses in the corral."

"They might be in that barn out back."

"Well, ya reckon we oughta sneak around there and take a look?"

"And if there ain't no horses there?"

"I reckon we go inside and see what's fer supper?"

Zack grinned back at Able before starting into the trees on a course that would keep them hidden right up to within about 50 feet of the barn. They went slowly, carefully, trying their best to avoid concentrations of the crunchy fallen leaves. It was quiet, save for the wind gently rattling the yellow leaves overhead, causing more of them to come floating down. At last, they were at a point where they could see the south end of the barn but not what was inside. They took a knee behind some sagebrush that was porus enough to where they could see the backside of the cabin and the end of the barn. There were two windows in the wall of the inn facing the barn. Being as close as they were now, they could hear voices inside. Zack sighed as the reality of their situation set in. "Sure as we go across this open ground to look in that barn they'll see us."

"Hell, they might be in there, ah drinkin' and not payin' attention ta what's goin' on out here."

Zack nodded. "They might, but if they ain't drunk and they do see us, and Frank recognizes us, they're likely ta come outta there guns a blazin'."

Able suddenly became angry, like his patience had been the grains of sand in an hour glass and the last of it had just run out, he said, "Ya know, we've buried Harley and the Sheriff and we've chased after these sonsabitches for quite some time now, I'll tell ya Zack, I just don't much give ah shit if they do come boiling outta that cabin. I say let 'em. Let's put an end ta this."

Able's demeanor was infectious. Zack came back, "Alright, you keep an eye out and I'll go check the barn,"

"No, I'll go. It's my idy ta risk twistin' their tail."

Zack broke off the debate and emerged from behind the brush in a crouched position, running towards the front of the barn. For a time, the stillness remained unbroken, the leaves swirling, floating erratically down from above and then, just as he opened the door, it ended. The voices from inside the cabin were loud and angry and garbled except for, "…damned O'Keefe's neighbor."

Zack stepped back out of the barn just as Frank and Gerald rounded the corner of the inn, pistols in hand. Zack hadn't heard the voices inside the cabin so he had yet to draw his pistol. Two shots rang out, one each from Frank and Gerald. One of the bullets splintered the wood in the door just above Zack's head, the other creased his right temple causing him to drop to the ground. And then a third shot sounded, a rifle shot from where Able was hiding. Frank went down, crumpled like a rag doll. Gerald on the other hand, thinking Zack was dead, shifted his aim to Able and fired. A split second later, Zack's bullet struck him just above his left ear. Gerald dropped as quick as if he'd been standing on the gallows and the trap door beneath him had suddenly opened. Zack struggled to get to his knees. The pain in his head was beginning to outpace his adrenaline to where it prevailed. He grimaced as he studied Frank and Gerald for any signs of life. Finally, satisfied they were dead, he got to his feet and began to stagger towards where Able had been hiding.

From his right, at the corner of the cabin came a voice, "Drop yer gun, Mister, or I'll blow ya ta hell."

Zack looked over. A fat man with a Winchester was leaning against the wall. He had a bead drawn on Zack. He hollered again, "If I haf ta tell ya again you can consider yerself dead."

Zack looked over at the fat man and then back to where Able should have been.

The fat man yelled again, "You simple sonovabitch, what part ah English don't you savy? Drop yer gun right now or I'm gonna kill ya."

And then from the sagebrush where Able was hiding came his voice, "Hold on, Mister, we're honest men."

The fat man kept his rifle pointed at Zack, but looked toward the clump of sagebrush. His eyes were fearful, frantic almost, as they searched the brush for the owner of the voice. Suddenly, he spotted the opening of Able's rifle barrel, down low, nestled back in the brush and grass. His reaction was spontaneous, "Don't shoot, please don't kill me." He then lowered his rifle to where the barrel was pointing towards the ground.

Zack hollered out to the man, "These fellas are rustlers and killers. We been on their trail for some time now. I'm sorry we happened ta catch up to 'em at yer place."

"I am too," said the fat man.

Abruptly, their eyes shifted to the sagebrush where Able was now standing. A dark red stain, up high in his left shoulder, immediately caught their attention. Zack started towards him, "How bad ya hurt?"

Able grimaced in pain. His left arm hung limp at his side while his right hand held his rifle, pointing towards the ground. He said, "I can't say fer sure, but it hurts purty damned bad."

Zack looked back at the innkeeper, who had not moved from the corner of the building, he called out, "Can we come inside?"

Hesitation paraded briefly across the man's face. His eyes darted to the two dead men on the ground in front of him and then back to the two wounded men still standing. It was clear that he wished none of them were there, that none of this had happened, at least not at his place he did, but what choice did he have, he said reluctantly, "Sure, come ahead on."

Zack holstered his pistol and took Able's rifle in order to free up his left arm so he could rest it across Zack's shoulders as they gingerly made their way towards the innkeeper. The man made no offer of help or sympathy. Instead, he stood there watching them hobble towards him until they drew near, whereupon he turned, without speaking, and went inside.

Able forced a weak laugh, "Friendly cuss, ain't he?"

Zack snorted and said in a low voice, "Yeah, he is."

The interior of the cabin was plain, it lacked a woman's touch. There were no decorations on the log walls except for a calendar from a mercantile in Baker City. It was one big room with a stove, wood box and shelves on the left side and three bunk beds on the right. In the middle of the room was a rectangular knotty pine table with chairs, made of the same wood, for eight people. Two coal oil lanterns, spaced evenly apart, sat on the table. Several brass spittoons were located on the floor around the table. Years of non-caring, drunken men having missed the spittoons were in evidence on the wooden planks beneath them.

The innkeeper went straight to one of the lower bunks. His back was still towards Zack when he said, in a tone that bordered on grumbling, "You can put yer friend down here."

Zack looked at the bed. It was akin to what they'd had in the Army. It was made of rough pine boards with a straw tick mattress. A couple of dark gray wool blankets were mostly wadded up on it. Zack left Able hanging on the upper bunk for balance while he straightened the blankets. He was about done when the innkeeper came again, "One ah yer friends outside slept here last night, but I reckon he ain't gonna need it tonight." And then he laughed.

The words flashed in Zack's mind, *what a sorry bastard.* He looked up at Able. His face was contorted in pain such that he didn't care what the man had said or where he was to lay. Zack helped him into the bunk. He called out, while examining Able's wound, "Could I trouble ya for a pan a water and some clean rags that I can make a bandage out of?"

The man frowned but said nothing before going to a waist high cupboard beneath some of the shelves at the opposite end of the room. Moments later he returned with a pair of Union Jack underwear. They were red and badly faded with several visible holes. He held them out towards Zack, "A fella left these here a while back. I was gonna take 'em for my own, but I reckon you can have 'em."

Zack took the underwear. At arm's length they smelled relatively clean. "Much obliged," he said. "And if I could git some water that'd be grand."

Able momentarily subdued his pain, he said, "Why is it I always git the ugly nurse?" He then purposely grinned, but just for an instant, as the pain took charge again.

Zack feigned insult. "That may be but the care will be top notch." And then he laughed while Able struggled to smile.

It took some time to clean and bandage Able's wound. He was lucky in that the bullet had gone clear through and did not appear to have broken any bones. On the other hand, however, he was in constant pain. Zack had bought him a couple of shots of whiskey from the German innkeeper, whose name was Anton Hohmeyer, but these did little good.

It was well after dark. Zack was just coming in from burying Frank and Gerald in the soft, silty ground near the river. He hadn't put them six feet down nor had he made them a cross. He was tired and his head throbbed from where the bullet had laid his scalp open. They got a rock with their name and the date etched on it. *If it was good enough for the Sheriff, its good enough for these two*, he'd said to himself. He sat down on the chair next to Able's bunk. He'd hoped that Able would be asleep, but he was not. He said, "how ya makin' it?"

Able flashed a weak grin, "If I could put this fire out in my shoulder, I'd be alright."

The worry already on Zack's face ratcheted up a notch. "You want more whiskey?"

Able closed his eyes and shook his head slightly. "Naw, it ain't sittin' well in my gut." He then looked up at Zack, "Can ya believe it, me turnin' down a free drink?"

Zack laughed briefly but quietly. "You need a sawbones."

"I 'spect so," said Able as he closed his eyes again to the pain.

Zack stood and went over to the stove where Anton was pouring himself a cup of coffee. As he neared the innkeeper, he allowed a brief void for him to inquire how Able was, but he did not. It was like the man was indifferent to the situation. Zack said, "Where's the nearest doctor?"

As if he needed to, Anton gripped his coffee mug with both of his big, meaty hands and took a noisy zip. Zack couldn't help but notice the coarse black hairs that grew between the joints on his fingers, but even more apparent was the fact he seemed to assign little importance to Zack's inquiry. Lowering the cup, he exhaled loudly. "Boise is probably yer best bet. It's a day's ride."

"My friend's in a lotta pain."

"I got plenty ah whiskey."

Zack shook his head. "It ain't agreein' with him. I wish there was a sawbones hereabouts, they'd give him some laudanum."

At the mention of laudanum, an uneasy 'gotcha' look flashed in Anton's dark eyes. It was such that he immediately took another drink of his coffee and looked away. His sudden change in demeanor, however, was not lost on Zack who blurted out, "You've got laudanum, don't ya?"

Anton's uneasiness deepened to shame. "It's hard ta come by."

"Maybe so, but my friend is hurtin'."

"It ain't cheap"

"How much?"

"I ain't got but the one bottle."

"Hopefully, that'll git him through."

Anton's look became distant, calculating, as he pondered the price. His shame appeared to be dissolving now that his secret was out in the open. Finally, he said, "Ten dollars."

Zack struggled to contain his anger. His first impulse was to draw his pistol and force Anton to give up the laudanum. As a private in the Army he'd made thirteen dollars a month and now, here he was being forced to pay almost a month's wages for a little bottle of medicine. He glared at Anton and scoffed. *He knows that he's got the upper hand*, he said to himself. And then, since he'd recovered Frank and Gerald's share from the sale of Harley's cattle, he turned away before fishing a wad of bills out of his shirt pocket.

Behind him, Anton laughed. "What's the matter? You afraid I'm gonna rob ya?"

Zack came around with the ten dollars in hand. He had no interest in bantering with Anton over the price of the laudanum, nor the fact that he would have kept it to himself had Zack not pressed him on it. He said, his voice indifferent and cold, "Here's yer money, where's the laudanum?"

Anton, sensing Zack's anger, kept quiet and went to the cupboard beyond the stove and knelt down. As he probed amongst the cans and bottles at the very back of the shelf his breathing became labored, owing to the fact his belly hung over his belt by about six inches. After some time, he found the right bottle and then grunted and puffed as he got to his feet. He held the bottle out to Zack. "Here ya go," he said, as if there was no animosity between them.

Zack took the bottle. He wanted to say to Anton, *you cudda saved my friend a lotta pain if you wudda brought this out a long time ago*, but he did not. Instead, he allowed his silence to speak for him as he went to Able's bunk and sat down on the chair beside it. He removed the cap and handed the bottle to Able. "Here, take ah swig ah this."

Able tipped the bottle up and took a couple of healthy swallows. He then made a sour face. "I believe whiskey tastes better 'n this stuff."

Zack grinned. "Well, maybe that's a sign it'll do ya some good."

It was a fitful night for Zack, even though he was reassured by Able's heavy breathing that progressed, at times, to snoring throughout the night. Zack, on the other hand, drifted in and out of sleep owing to the dull ache in his head and the dilemma of his circumstances. He knew that he couldn't leave Able in the care of Anton while he went after Bob Smith and Li Ming but, at the same time, it grated on him knowing that Smith was making off with the rest of the money that should've gone to Mabel O'Keefe. And then there was Li Ming. Anymore, she tied his mind in confused knots. He still felt a need to help her, but he was also attracted to her in the way a man is to a woman. And too, he couldn't divorce himself from a sense of obligation due to her having gave him the map with the X on it. For all she knew, that little creek held a fortune in gold and she gave it up to him. That had to mean something.

They had just finished breakfast, Able included, when Zack announced, "I believe I'm gonna go outside and have a smoke."

"Sounds tempting," said Able, "but I reckon I'm gonna lay down and let my parts mend."

"That's probably best. Maybe later take a little more laudanum."

Able nodded. "Yeah, that stuff is kinda the magic elixor. I'll tell ya, I ain't never been in such a deep fog."

"I'm glad ta hear it."

A sober look came to Able's face. "I'm sorry ta be holdin' ya up."

"Don't worry about it. We can only do so much."

"You should go on. I'll be alright here."

Zack glanced over his shoulder at Anton who was pouring hot water from a kettle into a big metal pan in preparation for doing the breakfast dishes. Facing Able, he lowered his voice, "I ain't real certain how you'd fare if it was just you and Anton here."

Able mustered a deliberate grin. "Well, I ain't gonna be running any footraces anytime soon, but I ain't as close to death's door as you think."

Zack shook his head. "I'll grant ya, yer more perky this mornin' than last night but my worry is what if you was to take a turn for the worse and I wasn't here. I ain't so sure that Anton would much give a hoot about it."

"He ain't no Clara Barton but if he just cooks, I believe I can tend to myself."

"That bandage needs ta be changed."

"So, you change it 'fore you leave. This Smith fella has already got a big head start. You allow him anymore and you'll never find him, Li Ming or Mabel's money. To my way ah thinkin' there's plenty ridin' on you stayin' or goin'."

Zack shot back. "Yeah, there is, you livin' or dyin'"

Able scoffed. "I ain't ready ta die."

"Most people aren't."

CHAPTER TWENTY

By mid-morning, Zack had succumbed to Able's urging to go on alone. It was not without considerable misgivings, however. The ride to Baker City was close to 70 miles, giving the naysayer in his mind plenty of time to berate him, *if you'd listened to Able and went to the marshal in Boise instead of coming to Oregon, none of this would've happened. Able would be ok and we'd be back home helping Shorty put up the rest of the hay.* But then, he rose to his own defense. He'd found in the barn, amongst Frank's gear, a .44-100 rifle. *Harley 'd be pleased ta know that we squared things with that scoundrel. He'd be glad ta know too that Mabel will have money, instead of nothing, to start over. Maybe move to a town somewhere.* And on it went, well into the second day, reshuffling their order, but the events that had put him where he was were never far from his mind.

He was a few miles from Baker City when up ahead he sighted a wagon coming towards him. It was a good two hundred yards away but Zack could still hear it rattling and clanking over the rutted road. The driver, an older man of medium build with a gray beard and a tan flat cap, was intermittently singing and cursing the four-mule team pulling it. As he came abreast of the wagon, Zack reined Biscuits to a halt. He called out in a cordial tone, "Afternoon to ya."

The driver brought the wagon to a stop. He had a can-tankerous look about him and said in a voice louder than necessary, "Headed to the big city, are ya?"

"I reckon, ain't never been there before."

"My recommendation to you is keep yer nose clean while yer there. That marshal they got is hardnosed. He don't tolerate nuthin."

Zack eyed the man briefly. He was not wearing a pistol but he had a Winchester lever gun leaning against the footrest and seat beside him. Zack came back, "You sound as if you've crossed paths with this old boy."

The man snickered. "There's been a time or two that John Barleycorn has caused me ta spend the night in the Marshal's hoosegow."

Zack grinned, but then went to what was on his mind. "You by chance haven't see a fella ridin' a gray horse that's got a Chinese woman with him have ya?"

The driver's face lit up. "I did, just this morning. They were tying their horses in front of the Logger's Retreat."

"That a saloon?"

"It is, right there on the main road goin' through town." The man paused briefly and then probed, "What's these folks ta you?"

The adrenaline was already flowing in Zack. He was anxious to go, to confront Bob Smith and put an end to all of this, one way or another. Nonetheless, he felt an obligation to answer the man's question. He came back, "The man is a scoundrel of the highest degree. He's a thief and killer."

Mild shock registered on the old man's face. "And the Chinese woman? She's a real looker. She could cause a man's head ta swivel right off if he wasn't careful."

Zack said simply, "She ain't broke no laws."

"Too bad she's with a fella like you say this guy is."

Zack nodded. "Much obliged for the information." And with that he nudged Biscuits onward at a good clip. The road, which had been carved out by early settlers in covered wagons, generally followed the most forgiving route through the sage covered hills. Within minutes, Zack had topped a pass that gave him his first sight of Baker City. It was a small town situated along the banks of the Powder River. What the old man had said about the marshal there echoed in his mind. *I should go look him up first thing*, he said to himself. *I don't need ta git crosswise with the law.* That intention was foremost in his thoughts as he entered town. There were the usual assortment of businesses and homes to either side of the road now turned Main Street, but so far none that was the Marshal's office. Suddenly, off to his left was an establishment that he did recognize. A faded white sign with big red letters whose paint was badly chipped read, LOGGERS' RETREAT. It rested above the door of a plain, single story log building with a tarpaper covered roof. Blue smoke was spewing lazily from its tin stovepipe. The windows to either side of the door gave the appearance of it being dark or, at best, shadowy inside like they were closed. But that was not the case, as tied to the hitching rail directly in front of the door was a gray horse and a sorrel. Zack's heart jumped into his throat. At last, he'd caught up to them. He guided Biscuits to a hitching rail in front of a doctor's office across the street and dismounted. The common sense, which only moments ago had been so abundant, was now in danger of deserting him. He stood there looking at the horses and the door to the saloon, his mind racing with what to do. *Bob Smith 'll have the advantage on me if I go waltzin' in there. I'll be goin' from daylight to a mostly dark room. Hell, by the time my eyes adjust to the light and I spot where he's at, I'll be dead.* He shifted his eyes up the street in search of the marshal's office, but there was no sign of it. *Dammit, if I go lookin' for that lawman they'll slip away, sure as I'm standin' here.* And then the saloon door opened and out stepped Li Ming, followed by Bob Smith. They did not go to their horses, but turned towards a diner just two doors away. It was in that instant that Li Ming, from the corner of her eye, caught sight of Zack standing next to Biscuits. She did not pause for long, but it was long enough for Bob Smith to see that Zack had drawn his pistol. To his credit, Smith shoved Li Ming to the side as he went for his gun.

Zack shouted, "Don't do it, Smith."

But it was like jumping off a cliff. There was no way for either one of them to reverse what was already in motion. Smith got as far as starting to aim his pistol when Zack pulled the trigger on his. Its roar and belch of smoke was followed by the sickening, but telltale slap, as the big slug buried itself in Smith's chest.

Li Ming screamed and began to cry as she watched Bob Smith stagger, while vainly attempting to return fire. Blood began to gurgle from his mouth before he slowly pitched forward into the dirt and horse manure. It was not as Zack had imagined it would be in his fantasy of how this meeting would go. Li Ming went to Bob Smith and knelt beside him, quietly crying. She reached out and touched his face, allowing her fingers to rest there a short time before getting to her feet. Zack had started towards her, but the sight of what she had just done stopped him in his tracks. He looked at her. She appeared lost or confused. And then people began to fill the street. Even the marshal, the non-existent marshal, bolted from a barbershop at the far end of town. He began to run towards where Bob Smith was lying dead. Some of the people just stood and stared, while others were walking quickly in the direction of the gunshot.

Zack could see the Marshal approaching, a fortyish looking man, of medium build with a black walrus moustache that was shaded by a wide brimmed gray Stetson. There was no mistaking him as his badge was evident on his dark suit coat and he had his pistol drawn.

Fear began to flood Zack's mind as he recalled the wagon driver's admonition. The circle of people around Bob Smith, Li Ming and Zack had gotten tighter causing the Marshal to holler out, "Let me through here."

Zack took a step towards the Marshal, thinking he would introduce himself when the Marshal suddenly pointed his pistol at him. "Hold on there, Mister. You the one that shot this man."

"Yes sir, I did. I –"

From the crowd came a voice offering up his take on what had happened. "This dead fella was mindin' his own business when this other guy comes along and just calls him out and shoots him. I was lookin out my window, Marshal. I seen it."

Zack eyes' were fixed in a hateful stare towards the bartender when he heard the Marshal cock his pistol and say, "Mister, I'm gonna need you to surrender your sidearm."

An immense rush of adrenaline hit Zack as the prospect of going to jail came to him. He made no move to give the Marshal his gun, but said instead, "I was intending to bring the man to you, Marshal. He's a thief and a murderer."

"What proof you got of that?"

After what he'd seen a short time ago, Zack was reluctant to bring Li Ming into this but he had no choice. He looked over at her. She had mostly stopped crying but her eyes were still watery and bloodshot. He said, "She knows. Li Ming knows the truth."

The Marshal looked at Li Ming and then back at Zack. He scoffed. "You go ta trial and all you got is the testimony of a Chinese girl you may be in big trouble, as I ain't so sure the judge would even allow it where it's concerning the murder of a white man."

Anger came to Li Ming's face. She'd retreated about ten feet from Smith's body after having knelt beside it earlier. She looked at the Marshal in a contemptuous way and then purposely went to the body and knelt again. Smith was wearing a dark green wool coat with button down chest pockets. She unbuttoned the left pocket and withdrew a wad of bills and held them up to the Marshal. She said, "He get this from cattle he steal and sell."

The Marshal took the money but looked doubtful. Before he could say anything, Li Ming folded back one of the coat flaps and reached in Smith's right breast pocket and then stood. She held out her hand, in it was a badge, it read: BOISE COUNTY SHERIFF.

The Marshal's eyes grew big as he picked up the badge.

Li Ming sniffed and took a breath as if to ward off anymore tears and then she looked at Smith and then back at the badge, she said, "he kill that man."

"You saw him do it?"

Li Ming nodded, "Yes, I right there."

"She's tellin' ya straight, Marshal," added Zack, "My partner and I buried him, or what was left of him, up along the South Fork of the Payette." And then he removed his hat to better show the wound he'd gotten at the inn. Pointing to the red and raw furrow across his temple he said, "Some friends of this fella gave me this a coupla days ago. They did worse to my partner. That's why he ain't here."

"They kill 'im?"

"Almost."

"And these other men?"

"I planted 'im behind a roadside inn next to the Snake River about two days ride south of here." Zack could see that the Marshal was weighing all that he'd heard, but he still had his gun pointed at him. Zack went on, "Marshal, this fella and his friends murdered my neighbor and stole his cattle. Me and my partner was just tryin' ta git the cattle back for his widow and kids. That's God's truth, Marshal."

The Marshal sighed before finally holstering his pistol. But then, out of the blue, he turned to Li Ming. "So what's yer part in this? It kinda sounds like you were in cahoots with these men."

A puzzled look came to Li Ming's face. "Cahoots? I no understand."

"You were part of their gang. You went along with what they were doing."

Panic filled Li Ming's eyes. "That not true. I have no choice." And then she added, pointing to Smith, "He win me in card game."

"He won you?" said the Marshal somewhat disbelievingly.

"She's tellin' ya the truth," said Zack. "It was a poker game over in Idaho City."

For Li Ming, there was no hiding her shame but she did not want to go to jail. "I saloon girl. Man who own my paper lose it to this man," she said pointing to Smith.

For the most part, the crowd had kept quiet so as to be able to hear all that the key participants had to say. But now a murmuring of whispers went through them until one rose above the others, "She's a whore."

Li Ming began to cry. Zack shot a hateful glance in the direction of the voice before looking at the Marshal, "You suppose we can finish this discussion in yer office?"

The Marshal nodded. "Follow me."

Zack felt as if everyone in the crowd was in judgement of him and Li Ming. The mostly male gathering was slow to make way as they sized them up. In a way, it was as if they were running an Indian gauntlet.

It was dark by the time they had rehashed to the Marshal's satisfaction, all of the events that had led up to Bob Smith getting killed in his town. The key to convincing him that they possessed the moral high ground was the Sheriff's badge and Li Ming's contract, which the undertaker had brought to him. Finally, with a recommendation they leave town, the two of them were allowed to go. For a time, they walked in silence towards their horses, seemingly all talked out from gaining their freedom and, surprisingly, the money from Harley's cattle. And then Zack said, hoping that it would not invite any critical discussion, "I reckon I better tend to my horse, yours too if ya like?"

"They are yours."

Zack looked over at Li Ming. Her offer had significant implications. She continued to walk with her eyes straight ahead. He said, "won't you need yer horse?"

They went on for another half dozen steps before Zack stopped her and forced her to look at him. He said, "My gut tells me there's something yer not tellin' me."

An anguished look came to Li Ming's face as tears welled up in her eyes. She said, "The man you kill, his real name Wiley Hocking. I know he do bad things, but he not all bad. He help me. Just like you try help me."

Zack shook his head. "I'm sorry Li Ming, but I can't see how running from the law is much of a life."

She looked up at him. Tears had begun to trickle down her cheeks. "We on our way to John Day. My uncle live there now. He give me place to stay, honorable work, new life. I go on stagecoach tomorrow."

"And yer friend, what about him?"

"He going come for me later, after he get ranch."

Feelings of betrayal and being foolish for having chased after her for this long suddenly came over Zack. They were getting the better of him until he recalled that he had recovered almost $3,000 for the widow O'Keefe. And then he took further solace in the fact that he already was part owner of a ranch and that he'd not been as desperate as Wiley Hocking to get it.

EPILOGUE

On the following morning, being the gentleman that he was, Zack had seen Li Ming off. She was sincere in thanking him for coming after her, even though she knew he may have had an ulterior motive. Regardless, Zack never saw her again after that day. Two days later, he arrived at the inn and the following day he and Able headed home. They did not talk to the U.S. Marshal in Boise as they had most of the money for the cattle and everybody involved in stealing them was dead. In Idaho City, they went first to file on the claim in Elk Meadows and then to Sam Wo's place to sign it over to him. Zack told him, *you git several fellas workin' it all next summer and I suspect you'll have enough money ta send Toby home.* And then came the part of their stop in Idaho City that neither of them wanted – going to see Sheriff Snyder's widow. They'd thought of sending a telegraph from Oregon, but that didn't seem right. On the other hand, it wasn't right that he was dead either. She was grief stricken. Zack's assurance that the Marshal in Baker City would be sending her the proceeds from selling her husband's killer's possessions was no comfort to her. For a time, they felt bad for having badgered the Sheriff about finding the rustlers. And then came their last stop before going home. Mabel O'Keefe had wanted to give them some of the money but they wouldn't take it. Later that fall, she sold the place and moved to Boise. They'd heard she became a school teacher.

When they finally arrived home, it had been dark. General had pitched a fit to get out of the cabin and come down to the barn. Close behind him was Shorty. True to form, he shouted out, *well, you boys finally decide ta come home now that me an' the General got the hay put up*. It was good that it had been dark, otherwise they would've seen the tears in Shorty's eyes.